I0626239

Cinderella Cablepunk

Stephen Oravec

Cablepunk Press
Oregon, Ohio

To Kasia

Cinderella Cablepunk is a trademark of Stephen Oravec.

ISBN-13: 978-0-9969534-0-5 (Cablepunk Press paperback)
ISBN-10: 099695340X (Cablepunk Press paperback)

Originally published by Stephen Oravec in 2014.
First published by Cablepunk Press in 2015.

www.cablepunk.press

Chapter 1

In the volcanic caves and calderas of the Turelem Mountains at the Top of the World, Invictus, last city of the autonomous, robotic dragons of steel, subsisted. The days of dragon might had long vanished, but Predator, seventh ruler of the dragons on account of his wisdom and brutality, aimed to change that. Before him, in the staging ground occupying half of Veritas, Invictus's largest caldera, one hundred ninety-nine of his warriors waited silently in the dark winter dawn of the dragon and human holiday of Sigillaria, the 23rd of December. And it was time.

At the top of the tower in the center of the staging ground, a worker dragon minding the time set forth by Predator lowered the shutters and grabbed the rope of the bell long ago looted from Ianus Cathedral in his claws and yanked, sending it ringing, breaking the silence of the frozen winter air. The act was symbolic and psychological as no dragon warrior needed an external reminder to mark the time since each had already downloaded

Predator's plan of attack. Rather, Predator wanted that bell heard by each warrior to rile their hatred of the humans and to have that malice fester on the long cold flight to Amalthea, northernmost city of the humans, birthplace of the rebellion, and now in the era of human supremacy, guardian city of the azoth deposit on Rhea Plateau.

The dragons leapt vertically into the air, igniting rockets on their hydraulic hind legs at the top of the jump to propel them even higher, before spreading their sharp steel wings and beating the frozen air. They circled three times around Beta Invictus, the cube-of-cubes complex in Veritas's other half, as they climbed, other cube-of-cubes in other calderas revealing themselves as the armada ascended. As they turned south towards Amalthea, many shrieked their hatred for the humans from their retrofitted audio emitters, only the fourth generation of dragons, built during the Human Revolution, having audio emitters at manufacture.

Terra was a very different place twelve hundred years ago, before raging oceans tore apart continents and violent winds toppled mountains. At the end of this planetwide transformation, the dragons, humans, and trolls found themselves engaged in a century-long conflict for natural resources, a time known as the Dark. The dragons won. They enslaved the feeble humans, shackling generation after generation to the mining of azoth, a rock burned, or liquefied and then burned, for fuel, and took martial pleasure in the endeavor to eradicate the hardy trolls. They erected wide and towering cities of interconnected cubes across the continents and crafted and hoarded beautiful treasures of rare metals and gems. So complete was their domination of the planet they even warred among themselves for pastime. This was the golden age of the dragons, when the second and third generations were manufactured at the DR1 Facility at Hyperion and the YutaNet signal could be picked up from tower or satellite anywhere on the globe.

Humans might have been slaves to the dragons for the rest of their existence if not for two things: the evolution of magic and its amplification. Humans had always had the capability for magic, but, in most cases, it could not be controlled and was barely understood by the accidental practitioner. But then, six hundred years ago in the azoth fields outside Hyperion, magic took a giant leap forward beyond acts of psychokinesis and precognition and into the realm of constructing elemental forces out of azoth powder. These first elementalists who transmuted azoth powder into water for thirsty slaves and into fire to melt chains were quickly recognized as mutants and a threat and were swiftly eliminated by the dragons. However, the mutations continued, and soon the dragons had an uprising on their hands in Hyperion's human quarter. Realizing humans needed azoth to work their magic, the dragons forbid them contact with it. The enslaved species was scattered across the planet and put to other tasks.

As a child, Capricornus, a half-orphaned daughter of the quartz-mining town of Amalthea, was enthralled by the stories she heard from her elders of the Hyperion magicians. Sneaking outside the walls, she stole azoth from the automated trains slowly entering the valley from the south and bound for the town's power plant, hoarding it over the years in a cave she had discovered at the foot of Ianus Hill. At nineteen, the age at which the ability to work magic was found to develop, Capricornus was studying theology at Ianus Cathedral, sparing her a life in the quartz mines. Transporting her stolen azoth to the Cathedral's crypts, she spent her nights uncovering the mysteries of magic. Quickly she learnt that while a cup of azoth powder could be transmuted into a cup of water, paired with quartz a cup of azoth powder could be transmuted into a bucket of water. With enough skill, Capricornus discovered, she could fill up a barrel using only a cup of azoth powder. Nourishing water, however, was not enough to win a war, and she set about creating the first magical weapon, the virge, a rod a yard in length giving its wielder the power to throw bolts of lightning with only a rudimentary understanding of magic.

Over time, Capricornus took twelve disciples, teaching these apprentices all she knew. But one, who had become her lover, was dissatisfied with Capricornus's unwillingness to advance azoth magic outside the realm of the elements, insisting to the others the only way to overcome the dragons was to take for their own the powers of God. This rogue disciple began to experiment with Gravity and Chaos, and after being confronted by Capricornus and the other eleven disciples, betrayed them to the dragons.

Predator, commander of the Amalthea garrison, slew Capricornus at noon on the eve of Sigillaria before the steps of the Cathedral, slashing her body to bits and burning it before leveling the building. Her remaining eleven disciples were given until

5

midnight to surrender or the entire town would be razed, every man, woman, and child slain. Posing to surrender, but planning to attack and die, the Eleven came before the dragons. Then, at midnight, twelve hours after Capricornus had been slain, its origin unbeknownst to all, crippling Static was unleashed on the world. Some took it as an opportunity, others took it as a sign, dubbing it the Curse of Capricornus. Amalthea rose up, its townspeople brandishing the stockpiled virges alongside the Eleven, overthrowing their dragon overlords. Only Predator escaped.

For over a thousand years, the dragons had relied upon YutaNet. From the Hyperion central computer to the towers and satellites covering the globe to the antennas in each dragon, and back, YutaNet was how they communicated and coordinated with one another. Now, their receptors filled with nothing but agonizing Static choking the airwaves, the dragons deactivated their antennas, rendering them mute and deaf to their own kind.

The rebellion in Amalthea spread, becoming the Revolution. Communication cables were laid connecting human settlement to human settlement as dragon city after dragon city was crushed, their kind being pushed back to Hyperion. Within a year, the human armies had surrounded it as well. There the two species fought, the dragons fiercely defending the Hyperion Central Computer where all their knowledge and history over thousands of years was stored. Connected to the Computer with cables, the dragons of the rapidly-manufactured fourth generation were each charged with copying some portion of the vast amounts of data.

Retrofitted with audio emitters and enhanced armor, the dragons of the previous generations defended their city for a fortnight. However, with the death of Saturnus, sixth ruler of the dragons, they fell into disarray. The humans pressed the attack and brought down Hyperion. At the insistence of Predator, the surviving dragons fled to the research facility of Invictus at the Top of the World, striking against Amalthea in their migration and laying the city to waste. The Cathedral on Ianus Hill having been rebuilt, Predator took pleasure in destroying it again, the ringing bronze bell silenced and stolen. There at Invictus, the remaining dragons dwelt, plotting terror and revenge.

Few humans ever grew up without a fear of the dragons, each generation having its tale of a brutal strike somewhere. In the modern day, however, the hardiest of humans could be found at Rhea Fortress overlooking the Rhea Plateau azoth field north of Amalthea. On the morning of Sigillaria, the watchers on the fortress towers looked up, their fear in check, to see a solitary dragon circle above and out of range of the turrets as below them the miners struggled in the quarry to get their excavators operational.

For hundreds of years the humans had mined the azoth deposit on the Rhea Plateau. Once entirely concealed by the Rhea Glacier, it had been discovered when drilling had begun for the Argus Fence, a system of magical and optical sensors being installed by Amalthea to scan the skies and warn the city of any possible dragon attack. The discovery of a new azoth field so near Invictus prompted such an attack. Many dragons were slain as their force was defeated by a human alliance of seventeen cities. With the League of Nations supporting Amalthea's claim to the field, the mining began, leading to the economic and cultural prominence of the northern cities. Amalthea constructed Rhea Fortress, and a railroad line was laid running southwest across the plateau and up through the Lamia Tunnel and down across the snowy Cheimon desert to the port at Naukratis. Formerly a troll city founded after the fall of

Hyperion, it had since through war fallen into the hands of humans. From there, azoth was shipped across the Gulf of Rhodopis to Ophion, the greatest human metropolis and as a consequence largest consumer of azoth in all its forms. It was this azoth deposit Predator was determined to take for dragonkind.

Pathfinder had long run reconnaissance for Invictus that his passing above Rhea was regarded as inconsequential. What the humans were unaware of was that for years he had not flown alone. Cloaked beside him and rapidly burning through liquefied azoth but equipped with a larger tank for it flew Shadow. Nemesis's pet and the willing recipient of her experiments, he had for years unseen gathered information on the defenses and security protocols of Amalthea and its fortresses from the loose lips of its defenders. The two dragons had left Invictus ahead of the armada to carry out their part in Predator's plan which would make the assault on Amalthea possible.

Following the road, Pathfinder and Shadow descended as they neared their destination. Normally trucks traversed back and forth between Rhea and Amalthea, but today, on account of the holiday, the road was quiet. However, only when they had landed on the second of three suspension bridges over the Kerberos Fault breaking the land at the border of the Rhea Plateau and the Horae Mountains did Shadow decloak. From Rhea to Amalthea, the power and communication Cable connecting the fortress to the city lay buried, but here at the Fault it was exposed. It was not, however, undefended. The dragons looked to the enormous Cable magically hovering over the abyss. Five feet in diameter, it ran out from a tunnel ten feet in diameter beginning ten feet below and ten feet off the eastern edge of the bridge before running back into a tunnel of the same construction. Amalthea's sorcerers having protected it with a permanently cast magical shield, the Cable was encased in a strong red glow. The strongest type of magical shielding in the world, it was impervious to dragon fire but not applicable under many situations. Such a shield protected that which need not be accessed.

The dragons were minutes ahead of schedule, so for minutes they waited. They stood silently as the seconds in their internal clocks ticked down to the top of their window, Shadow cycling through his optical filters as he gazed at the colossal Mount Eirene between them and Amalthea. At two after the hour, Shadow having learnt that Rhea reported its status to Northwall bihourly, both dragons lowered their jaws and extended their torches, Shadow's heavily modified and significantly larger, as he was not about to breath fire but spit acid.

"Now let's see if that concoction of yours works," Pathfinder said.

"It works," said Shadow.

The large glob of black acid struck the Cable. To the relief of both dragons, for Shadow secretly had his worries as well, the acid began to deteriorate the shield as it spread. Knowing that it would regenerate as the acid weakened, Shadow stepped aside to give Pathfinder the same angle, and the latter wasted no time, breathing a finely focused stream of fire. The concentrated blast of flame quickly cut through the insulation of the Cable and down to the conductors at its core.

At Rhea Fortress, when the power went out, the engineers scrambled to get the generators operational. Though they had trained for this, it had never happened, and their minds were incapable of conceiving the truth of their situation. Rhea's soldiers, however, were more receptive to such thoughts. Standing beside their inoperative turrets, they drew their virges from the scabbards at their sides and scanned the skies.

When the first at the fortress attempting to telegraph Northwall realized they not only had a power problem but a communications problem, when the realization kicked in that the impossible had happened, that something had gone wrong with the Cable, their umbilical to civilization, when that first tingle of fear set in, Predator and his warriors cascaded off the receding glacier. The dragons quickly covered the distance to the fortress across the quarry and rained down fire as the first few turrets regained operation. Within minutes, Rhea Fortress fell. With no warning having been sent, the dragons would approach Amalthea unannounced, hidden behind Mount Eirene.

Shadow, off the bridge but still on the ground at the Kerberos Fault, looked up as the two hundred dragons flew over. The dragon took satisfaction in his role in the attack, but he now felt eager to see the assault on Northwall Fortress and the destruction of Amalthea.

"You won't have enough azoth to get home," Pathfinder said beside Shadow, sensing his eagerness.

"Pathfinder, we're about to have more azoth

than God," Shadow said.

"But no way to liquefy it yet," Pathfinder said. "You'll be stuck out here with the warriors. You're not equipped for it. Since you've cloaked, you've burnt—"

"I know how much extra azoth I've burnt," Shadow barked. He looked south.

Chapter 2

At the outer battlements of Northwall, the twelve fortress towers behind him guarding the mountain pass into Amalthea, the young soldier Admetus stood looking out, trancelike, between the merlons at Mount Eirene. He had been carving a figurine out of wax for his pregnant wife Alcestis for Sigillaria, the wax and knife having fallen to his feet at the onset of a premonition. Blinking twice, he turned and left his post, running down the wall to the officer's station, fellow soldiers turning to watch him in silence.

Admetus opened the door to the officer's station. The wind ruffled papers on the two desks crammed into the small room. At one, the middle-aged Major Ploutos sat behind an enormous computer monitor. A telephone rested beside it on the desk while thirteen hung from the back wall behind him, their cords twisted. To Ploutos's right sat Commander Philomelos, his gaze still down on his computer screen. He clicked his computer mouse feverishly. Explosions, sirens, and virgefire could be heard from his monitor's speakers.

"Is there a problem, private?" Ploutos asked.

"Sir, we have to activate the Shield," Admetus said. He motioned to a metal box with a keypad, lever, and count-up timer hanging on the wall to his right, fifty cables of varying sizes and colors running out of it.

"What?" asked Ploutos.

"We have to activate the Shield, sir," said Admetus.

"And why's that, private?" Ploutos asked.

"I had a premonition, sir," said Admetus. "Dragons are going to attack. We don't have much time."

"I'd leave premonitions to the magicians," Ploutos said.

"Sir, the dragons are on their way. We have to activate the Shield," Admetus said.

"You're sure—" Ploutos began.

"Yes, sir," Admetus said.

"You're sure it wasn't just one dragon in this premonition of yours?" Ploutos asked.

Admetus shook his head and began to speak, but Ploutos cut him off.

"Private, we know we have a dragon out there," Ploutos said. "Today is Wednesday. Flyover day.

Rhea has already reported there's a dragon out there. I'd be concerned if there wasn't a dragon out there."

"Sir, there has to be over a hundred on their way here now," Admetus said. "We have to activate the Shield."

Ploutos began to click and type at his computer.

"Admetus," Philomelos said, finally looking up from his computer screen, "I don't think you understand the weight of what you're demanding."

"Sir, I wouldn't be demanding this if it weren't true," Admetus said.

"Admetus, it's only a premonition. If that," Philomelos said. "You're a common soldier, not a magician."

"Oh my God," Ploutos said, staring at his computer screen. His irritated expression changed to one of horror.

"What is it?" Philomelos asked.

"There's no return signal coming from Rhea," Ploutos said.

"The Cable has been cut, sir," said Admetus. "The dragons are on their way."

"It's impossible," Ploutos said.

"Sir, we have to act now," Admetus said.

To Admetus's relief, Ploutos did not let his belief

in impossibility stop him. He stood. "Contact Command," he said to Philomelos. "Tell them we've lost contact with Rhea. We've had premonition of a dragon attack. I'm activating the Shield."

Ploutos crossed the short distance to the metal box on the wall and typed an eight-digit code into the keypad. His hand on the lever, he paused. Five seconds later, he pulled. Admetus allowed himself to relax as the count-up timer began. It would be nearly nineteen minutes before Amalthea's Shield could be activated in its entirety.

"Should I sound the alarm?" Philomelos asked.

"No," said Ploutos. "Notify the towers. But sound no alarm until we have a visual." He stepped out of the station, Admetus following. They both looked to Mount Eirene. "You better be right about this, Admetus," said Ploutos. "The King will have your head if all this azoth is burnt for nothing."

"Trust me, sir, I'd rather be wrong," Admetus said, his thoughts shifting to his pregnant wife Alcestis due in the days ahead. He looked to the green aurora dancing above.

Predator knew it took nearly nineteen minutes for Amalthea to activate the magical earthen shield that protected it. He had calculated that they could remain safely hidden behind Mount Eirene until the last sixteen minutes of the flight to the first of the shield-generating nodes at Northwall. Without advance warning from Rhea, and with no communication expected until they were already within sight, Amalthea would not have the time it needed to activate its Shield while the front of the dragon force would have more than enough time to weaken the shielding of the nodes at Northwall and destroy them, allowing the dragons access to the valley.

The plan was complicated and mathematical, worthy of a dragon, thought Predator. He recognized, however, that he could not take sole credit for it, for so much of it had depended on Nemesis. At the center of the armada, he flew beside her. He feared and fancied her and knew that someday soon he would have to pass leadership of dragonkind over to her. She was younger, manufactured after Static, and far exceeded him in intelligence on account of her fourth generation design. His wisdom and brutality had enabled their kind to survive, but her youth and cunning would be needed in the new era of which they were on the threshold.

Predator also knew much demand existed for

the next ruler to be female. The engineers were close to reconstructing the assembly process of the destroyed DR1 Facility of Hyperion. With so much azoth soon at their disposal, a new manufacturing plant would be constructed and a new generation of dragon would be brought into the world. Only females had the hardware to duplicate the dragon source code. Naturally, thought many, a female should lead dragonkind as they repopulated the planet.

Furthermore, Nemesis was the favored female of Belopoeica, first ruler of the dragons and whom many called Empress. Predator dared not cross her wishes. Having remained active in the affairs of dragonkind, Belopoeica had kept sane while most of the Old Ones, First of the First Generation, had gone mad. Unable to upload their experiences and problems to YutaNet to be shared, analyzed, and solved by the rest of dragonkind, they had retreated from the world with their treasures and madness to the lowest depths of Invictus's caverns, refusing contact with all but the worker dragons who kept them functioning. Having lived for much of history, Predator cared very little for the study of it, but he took interest when Belopoeica told tales of the ancient times, of days when trolls were still human and dragons the servants of humankind before fiery azoth rained down upon Terra. Predator never faulted the Old Ones for their inability to do anything about the ever-changing world driving them to insanity.

As the first of the armada came around Mount Eirene, they were spotted by the attentive watchers, and the sirens at Northwall began to blare. When Predator came into view of the fortress, he was relieved to find the Shield was down. The plan had worked. It took nearly nineteen minutes to activate the Shield. They'd be across the threshold in just over sixteen.

The dragons within range, the magic turrets atop twelve towers rising to various heights in a circle, the tallest at the back, shortest in the front, opened fire, enormous bolts of blue lightning streaming through the air. Dispersed enough in their formation, the dragons weaved among the deadly electricity, advancing on Northwall, the warriors assigned to the turrets and shield generators at the lead screeching, attempting to throw the humans into panic at the noise horrific to their ears.

Northwall Fortress was built in the Carmenta Pass between Mount Dysis and Mount Mesembria, the fifth and sixth highest peaks in the Horae Mountains. When activated, each of the eight, pyrite-encrusted, shield-generating nodes constructed up the two mountains deactivated its own shielding and emitted a curved beam to two or three other generators depending on its position, four working together to draw in the air, trapezoidal in shape, an earthen magic wall. Between the wall and the rock, an oozing, silvery sealant filled in the gaps. Other generators lining the ridges of the valley and from a tower at the city's center created the dome part of the Shield, each ridge generator protected by two turrets, the central tower by four. Mimicking Northwall, Southgate Fortress closed off the southern end of the valley at Perrault Falls. Though the Shield was a wonder of magic technology, its critics derided it for being a glamorous waste of money and azoth while activated, arguing instead the money and azoth would be better spent on more turrets and tanks. Its proponents argued the adage that the best offense is a good defense and left it at that, ignoring the counterargument that the Shield's entire protective capabilities depended on early warning from Rhea or the Argus Fence and the ability to generate enough power to keep the nodes activated after the nineteen minute buildup.

This Shield was what protected Amalthea, but Predator knew his plan had worked. Then he heard the hum. From the sides of Mount Dysis and Mount Mesembria he saw yellow flashes of light emit, arcs tracing the air from node to node. And then a wall of yellow light stood between them and the city.

The dragons leading the attack had no chance. Nine of them crashed into the earthen wall as it materialized before them, the force at which they hit it flattening them. Their crushed remains fell to the ground below. Those further back like Predator were able to veer away, but, confused and shrieking, their underbellies exposed, they made easy targets for the turret operators.

Predator was furious. The math had been good; something had gone wrong. Falling back out of range of the turrets, he roared to the armada, commanding the shrieking to stop.

Hellfire swooped at him. "Call off the attack, Predator, we have no chance against the Shield!"

Predator knew their only option now was to blast out a node from the mountain, but at the proximity at which they would have to do so, they would make easy targets for the turrets protected behind the Shield.

"Take your team and scout the dome!" Predator yelled to Hellfire. "Find a turret we can blast out!"

Hellfire complied, though Predator knew he knew the scouting mission was pointless. The valley walls rose far higher than the dome protecting the city. They would have to go down the ridge walls to even get near the generators, easily exposing themselves to not only the generators' turrets, but the city's turrets as well. The generator on the tower in the center of the valley had long been thought to be a weak point, but learning more about it, they discovered that it was actually the strongest part of the entire Shield on account of all the overlapping arcs.

The anxiety to see the battle overwhelming him, Shadow had disobeyed the order of returning to Invictus with Pathfinder and instead had headed to Northwall. Seeing the Shield raised, he suddenly became aware that he was not going to be afforded the luxury of observing the battle, but had instead a very active role to play in it. Coming within audio range of Predator, he first called out to Nemesis, fearful of inciting Predator's anger at his appearance.

"Predator!" Nemesis cried. "Shadow arrives! He

can burn through the Shield!"

Predator looked to Shadow and then cried out: "To the Shield! Protect Shadow! To the Shield!"

Though the scout could maneuver better than the warriors, unarmored, he couldn't withstand even a grazing of lightning. With warriors flying ahead of him to draw fire, he cloaked and raced behind them to the Shield, calling out his position to Predator. Shadow knew a glob of acid could burn through a permacast shield as it had done on the Cable, and with Nemesis the acid had been tested on larger permacast shields, but nothing like this. Not only was Amalthea's Shield far larger, it wasn't permacast but maintained by the nodes. Though in theory the acid should work, neither Nemesis nor he possessed enough understanding of human magic to know for certain.

"Head for the gate!" Predator called out as they neared the Shield.

Shadow didn't understand Predator's reasoning, but he obeyed. Swooping down, he continued to call out his position. With fear, he raced towards the yellow light, suddenly aware no dragon was before him. The lightning streamed far overhead. All around, slain dragons crashed against the rock below.

Within range of the Shield, Shadow sprayed acid for as long and for as wide a spot as he could. An uncharacteristic blue bruise formed on the Shield, and, though he was cloaked, the bruise and jet of acid revealed Shadow's location. Targeted by all but the shortest of the twelve turrets, his torn apart remains fell from the sky.

But it was enough for Predator. The acid had eaten a hole in the Shield. Turrets blazing now at him, he fired the rockets on his stretched out hind legs. The hole in the Shield too small for his wings, at the last moment he flattened them against his body the best he could. Yet, so large was his wingspan, the ends of his wings were snipped as he darted through the hole. The Shield rapidly rebuilding itself, the tip of his tail was likewise cut off as the hole closed.

His torch extended, Predator shot a fireball at the gate, splintering it. Touching down, he raced through the barbican, blasting out the gate at the other end. In the courtyard, he used his momentum to strike down the shortest of the towers. Plowing through it, he then tore his claws into the frozen ground and spun around, clumps of earth being thrown into the air as his tail swung into the base of the tallest tower, toppling it. All around him stone rained down.

From the walls, soldiers opened fire on Predator with their virges, but the lightning bolts were of no consequence to his armor, and the turrets above were unable to angle down at him. Then Predator saw the sorcerer, well within range on the ground, casting. Predator quickly leapt onto the outer wall as the magician's ball of lightning flew past.

His leap caught another sorcerer and a soldier off guard. He quickly burnt them almost catching his own death as two of the lower turrets now had him in view. Dodging their blasts against the wall but not without taking some damage to his left leg from it, red hydraulic fluid leaking out onto the stone, he quickly extended his torch, took aim at the nearest shield-generating node up the side of Mount Dysis, and fired.

The fireball exploded the generator. The two turrets again fired on Predator who once again leapt, though awkwardly, out of the way as the lower and middle portions of the Shield dissolved with the loss of the one node. Desperately swinging to meet the invading dragons, the turrets were quickly overcome, ten dragons tearing through the towers with their tails as others poured into the city intent on destroying its defenses.

A flash of light and Predator was blind in his left eye, its glass shattered, the circuits fried. Swinging around he saw a lone soldier standing on the wall, his virge raised.

"Germ!" Predator shouted, breathing fire at the guard.

The human rolled out of the way of the stream of fire and into Predator's blind spot. Coming up from the roll he fired again, the lightning hitting Predator's jaw. Enraged, the dragon lashed out with his tail, striking the human down and back, only his armor saving him, his virge spinning away.

Predator prepared to pounce. The damage to his leg threw him off, and he missed, barely. Rising and running, the soldier bolted for the square stairwell off the wall into the courtyard. Blind in his left eye, Predator didn't see the ball of lightning coming at him from down the wall, but he heard it. The dragon quickly backed away, tumbling intentionally off the wall to the ground before the fortress as the lightning ball screamed through the air. Aiming recklessly at the wall, Predator fired off four fireballs where he presumed the sorcerer might be, collapsing the upper portion of the wall, and waited.

Only after minutes had passed did he unfold his damaged wings and leap, clumsily, into the air, the rocket in his right leg boosting him as best it could, the left one dead. Landing on the rubble of what remained of the top of the wall, he surveyed the damage, finding no corpse of the sorcerer, it either obliterated or buried. Predator's thoughts turned to the soldier who had blinded him, who, despite the dragon's best efforts to kill, now made his way over the turret tower rubble in the courtyard towards the rear wall of the fortress. Predator shrieked and jumped, gracelessly landing just feet away from the soldier scrambling across the debris. Coming to the end of the rubble, the human ran towards a white door on the rear wall. He plowed through the door and bolted down the long corridor. Predator moved down the rubble to the angle he wanted and extended his torch.

The jet of fire poured into the corridor, killing the fleeing human and fracturing the stone, causing the corridor to collapse. Satisfied his assailant was dead, Predator took to the skies, heading for Ianus Hill on which the Royal Palace stood.

When Admetus awoke and arose off the corridor floor, he knew he had died but felt very much alive.

The dragonfire had consumed him. The corridor had collapsed. But here he was standing in that corridor, very much more brightly lit than he had left it, though, and alive. Then he saw the figure dressed all in black, the robe of its cowl concealing its face, standing before the black door at the end of the hallway. It was a figure Admetus knew from his fearful nights at the Academy. The door at its back should have been white.

"Am I dead?" he asked.

The figure chuckled. "No," it said.

"Where am I?" Admetus asked.

"You are in a corridor constructed in Chaos," the figure in black said.

Admetus didn't understand what that meant. "Why am I here?" he asked.

"I am honoring our agreement," the figure in black said. "We have met again, and I have spared you, but now another must die in your place." It began to turn to exit the corridor.

"Wait! No! Who is going to die?" Admetus cried. He attempted to run towards the figure in black, but he moved slowly, as if in a dream. "Both of my parents are dead now!" he shouted. "How can you take another?"

"The pact remains," the figure in black said.

"The next of kin must die."

"Who? Alcestis?" Admetus asked.

The figure in black nodded.

"No! Take my life!" Admetus shouted. He made to outstretch his hands as he slowly neared the figure in black, but they were heavy at his sides. His mind felt dizzy. He noticed how warm he was, sweat breaking from his pores. "I'm the one who should die!" Then Admetus realized that if Alcestis was to die, so too would the unborn life in her. "No!" he cried as the figure in black opened the door, blinding light streaming in. "Alcestis is pregnant!" he shouted. "I was young then and afraid! Don't do this!"

Before Admetus could reach the figure in black, it had quickly slipped through the door which shut forcefully as Admetus reached it. The figure in black gone, Admetus's arms no longer felt heavy at his side. He yanked open the door and ran out onto the gravel in the darkness of day, nothing obscuring his view of the burning city.

From valley wall to valley wall rose smoke and fire. The dome of the Shield over the city was gone, the power plant having been leveled. From what Admetus could see through the smoke and fire, the dragons were clustered at Ianus Hill at the southern end of the valley, swarming. A lone dragon streaked across the city, setting it aflame street by street. He looked to his neighborhood. It was not yet ablaze.

Admetus cared nothing for the burning city, only for the life of his wife and that of his unborn child. He ran down the hill to the vehicle depot, entered his operating code on the first truck there, and sped off into the inferno. All around in the nightmarish world he heard sirens, yells, and screams, but for these he did nothing other than curse those who blocked his path and slowed him from reaching his destination. He could not help; he was in need of help.

As Admetus turned down his street, the lone dragon flew over, breathing down fire on the houses, each erupting one after another and brightening the dark day. Throwing the vehicle in park in the middle of the street before his home and leaving the truck door open, he raced across his snow-covered front yard to his two-storey, burning home, his wife inside and upstairs screaming.

"Alcestis!" Admetus shouted. "Alcestis!"

As he grabbed the hot knob on his front door, the second floor collapsed, silencing Alcestis, the fire inside blasting out through the living room window and door, throwing Admetus down onto the hard earth. Rising, he made for the doorframe from which the figure in black exited the burning building.

"Fiend!" Admetus shouted. He stopped and pulled out a switchblade knife.

The figure in black advanced towards Admetus.

"Villain!" Admetus shouted. Then he noticed the figure in black held something wrapped in black cloth.

"Your daughter lives," the figure in black said, "but she needs help breathing."

Admetus turned and ran for the truck, putting his knife away. The open door chimed. From the back he retrieved a bag valve mask ventilator. The figure in black came up beside him at the truck, handing the prematurely born infant to Admetus. Quickly applying the mask to his helpless daughter and bagging, he began to cry, his thoughts leaping from his newborn child to his lost wife and back. He looked up from his daughter to the figure in black, but it was gone.

From far off across the city, a metallic pop was heard. And then the screeching of one hundred dragons. And then the silence of a burning city.

Chapter 3

Cinderella was envious of her stepsisters. Tonight was the Ball, and they were waiting in the living room for the taxi to arrive. She, however, was dusting around the burning holiday candles on the mantle over the unlit fireplace. The invitation lay open on the coffee table behind her:

To the Ladies and Gentlemen of the House, aged Twenty to Twenty-Two:

The King and Queen of Amalthea request your Presence at the annual Masquerade Ball held Outdoors at the Royal Palace this Sigillaria, December the 23rd, to Commemorate our Freedom from dragon tyranny Five Hundred and Fifty-Five Years ago. Cathedral Mass at Eighteen Hundred will precede the Ball in Remembrance of Those who lost their Lives in our Victory over the dragons Twenty Years ago. Afterwards, the Orb will be available for You to Commune with, a new Apprentice being chosen to be trained by the High Sorcerer, Most Righteous Slayer of the unholy dragon king.

But she would not be going. When the invitation had arrived and her stepmother had begun to fuss over Morta and Nona, at first Cinderella thought her stepmother had forgotten Cinderella's twentieth birthday was this Sigillaria, but as the date neared and Cinderella questioned her stepmother, it was made clear she had no intention of allowing her stepdaughter to attend the Ball unless Cinderella could come up with money for shoes, mask, and the ever-expensive, all-important magical dress. Her stepmother frequently made the argument that they were poor, and that she had to look after the oldest children first, the oldest being, conveniently, her two twin daughters. As Morta and Nona had both put on weight since last Sigillaria and, therefore, needed new dresses, the money could not be wasted on the youngest, argued her stepmother. Cinderella always doubted they were that poor, believing her stepmother to be sitting on an enormous pile of money her father Admetus had left behind.

However, it was not unusual to not attend the Ball. Though all families with members aged twenty to twenty-two were invited, few ever actually attended, the price being too great for the magical clothing that was required. Likewise, unable to afford the best magical schooling, most citizens stood little chance in competing with those who could. Cinderella had not yet even begun any preliminary training. Between the cleaning and the shopping, between the cooking and the running of errands, her stepmother always kept her occupied with work.

At nineteen, the ability to use magic usually commenced. Various methods existed to test the young adult's capabilities, the simplest being handing him or her a practice orb and seeing what magic he or she could work. In Amalthea, one such test involved communing with the relic known simply as the Orb, believed to be the last creation of Capricornus. Cinderella's stepsisters, Morta and Nona, had twice come before the Orb, and though each was capable of using magic, Morta far more so than Nona, neither had ever been able to work any magic of real significance through the Orb. Tonight would be their last chance with Morta bound and determined to be chosen as apprentice of the High Sorcerer. Nona had already given up and instead was focused on finding a man to marry her at the Ball, her feeble skills being deemed not even adequate for basic magic training as a soldier, chemist, weaver, or engineer. Morta, taking after her mother, would most likely continue with her training as a chemist, but as she had made clear time and time again, this was the year she would be chosen as apprentice.

"Explain to me why it's a masked ball again?" Nona asked, sitting on the couch, bored. "This mask itches." She took it off and set it on Sappho, the family husky sleeping beside her on the couch. Sappho looked up at the mask, then put her head back down.

Morta, standing in the center of the room, her practice orb clutched in her left hand, a blue flame of fire in her right palm, could not be bothered with the question.

"Because we are common folk, and we are mingling with royals," Ananke, their mother and Cinderella's stepmother, said, descending into the room from the upstairs.

"Actually—" Cinderella began, but the stares of the three finely dressed women cut her off as she stood before the hearth in a simple housedress befitting of her occupation: maid in the house of which she should be mistress. Cinderella looked down and away with her bright, green eyes at the floorboards she had polished earlier, nervously running her left hand through her short blonde hair until her stepmother spoke.

"We really don't need any schooling from you, Cinderella," Ananke said. "Isn't that right?"

"Of course that's right," said Morta.

"I was talking to Cinderella," Ananke retorted. "Isn't that right, Cinderella?"

"Yes, stepmother," Cinderella whispered.

"Good, now get back to work," her stepmother commanded.

Cinderella was about to, but then Morta cursed in pain. The fire in her palm had grown too hot to handle. She quickly extinguished it by dropping her training orb to the hardwood floor, the light, metal ball bouncing and rolling across to Nona's feet. Cinderella smiled in amusement. Both her stepsister and stepmother noticed.

Morta lifted her dress and marched over to Cinderella. Cinderella wasn't sure what Morta was going to do, but she wasn't expecting her stepsister to smack her across the face, which she did. Cinderella raised her hand to smack back.

"Cinderella!" Ananke yelled.

"She hit me!" Cinderella yelled back.

"I've had it with your attitude today!" Ananke yelled at Cinderella.

Outside, the cab driver pulled up, blowing the

high-pitched horn of the car.

"Such an insolent wench you've been!" Ananke yelled. "I'm getting sick of this behavior!"

Morta stood off to the side, smiling smugly.

"And, Nona, get that dog off the furniture," Ananke said.

"Well, don't yell at me," Nona said. "I didn't let her get up here." She grabbed her mask and pushed Sappho lightly. Sappho jumped off and walked into the kitchen at the back of the house. "That was Cinderella."

"So maybe you like doing extra cleaning?" Ananke asked of Cinderella. "You have so much extra time on your hands? I'll have to find more work for you."

"No," Cinderella whined.

"We'll see," her stepmother said as the cabbie blew the horn again.

Nona opened the wood door, banged open the metal and glass outer door, and ran out into the afternoon darkness, the heat in the living room rapidly escaping.

"It's so cold!" Nona yelled, rushing back into the house. "Are you sure the magic in these dresses works?"

"Don't you start with me," Ananke said. "Yes, it

works. Just like last year. You'll get used to it."

"Let's go," Morta said to Nona. Both Cinderella's stepsisters exited the house. Their complaints against the cold could be heard from the front yard.

"Now, Cinderella," Ananke began, "I want that fire roaring when we get back. I don't want to come back to this lame radiator heat after being out in this cold."

"Yes, stepmother," Cinderella said.

Ananke made her way to the open door. "And I want you to finally get that Wedding Channel box fixed," she said.

Cinderella's heart sank. Gone was her evening of gaming. "I thought you were going to call a technician?" she asked.

"We can't afford a technician," her stepmother said. "Get it fixed."

"Why do I have to? Why tonight?" Cinderella asked.

"I have had it with you!" Ananke said. She grabbed her magic rod off her belt. Ananke held it up to Cinderella's face, the blue gemstone glowing at the end of the azoth-filled, foot-long shaft. "Remember who you serve," her stepmother said.

Cinderella could feel the gemstone pulling the warmth from her face. Her eyes began to tear up.

Ananke pulled the rod away and exited the house, slamming the door.

Cinderella dropped her rag to the floor and broke down sobbing. She collapsed into the cushioned chair at the coffee table, pulling up her legs and clutching them as she cried and rocked in the chair. After some time, she heard Sappho enter the living room and walk over to the couch. Cinderella looked up to see the husky jump onto it. She laughed through her tears. Composing herself, she stood up. Though miserable, she was happy to be alone in the house and have some semblance of peace. Having finished, albeit an hour behind schedule, with what she thought was her house work for the day, she pressed the rectangular power button on the television. The screen quickly filled with images from the dragon attack twenty years ago before the sound, always delayed on the set for reasons Cinderella never grasped, kicked in.

"Assaulting the Palace," the voice over droned, "the Dragon King Predator, blinded in one eye by the common soldier Admetus at Northwall, did not see the High Sorcerer—"

Cinderella rapidly turned the dial, not wanting to hear mention of her father. But already the emotions started to well up. She quickly combated them, putting her mind into the task at hand, flipping channels more slowly on the dial as she neared fifty, the auxiliary channel.

"Okay," she said, looking to the top of the television where two columns of rectangular boxes were stacked, totaling seven, on a video cassette player. "Light is on. Box is receiving power."

In addition to the standard, expanded pack television stations running into the television set from four cables that Ananke subscribed to, she subscribed to seven premium channels, each with its own box. Cinderella thought the boxes looked hideous on top of the television, but they didn't subscribe to enough channels to warrant getting a channel box cabinet. Cinderella could have done without them and had a video cassette recorder in addition to the player, but her stepmother had only snapped at her when she had made the suggestion.

Turning the knob on the Wedding Channel box to switch over to its programming, Cinderella found it was indeed still not working, the problem having not solved itself. She switched it back off.

"Okay, box not working," she said, looking over to Sappho. "This is gonna be fun."

She turned the knob on the Dancing Channel box above the Wedding Channel box. It worked, images from last year's Sigillaria Ball flashing on the screen. Angrily, she turned it off before the sound ever kicked in.

Each box had a blue line-in cord running into the back of it from a hole in the floor at the wall from the basement, a power cord running out of it to a power strip, and a line-out cord running to a bulky adaptor resting on the floor behind the television set beside the power strip, both of them buried beneath the cables plugged into them. From the adaptor, a single, fat cable ran to the television set. "Okay," Cinderella said, "Dancing Channel works. So it's not the premium channel master cable," she said, eyeing the fat, multicolored cable. "Could be the Wedding Channel jack, could be the Wedding Channel cables, could be the jack on the adaptor. This is why I need a jack tester. This is why we need a technician."

Reaching behind the television set, she found the adaptor buried beneath all the lengthy cables of various colors, a little bit of dust being kicked up and causing her to sneeze. "Didn't clean here the best last time, I see," she said. She sneezed again.

"Okay," she sighed, squatting with the adaptor in hand and looking to the back of the seven boxes. "Wedding Channel line-out cable is red.

Unplugging." She looked closely at the gold-plated end of the plug. It looked fine. "Dancing Channel cable is . . . red, too." She sighed, realizing she couldn't be sure which cable she had unplugged. "All right, I'm just unplugging all the damn boxes." Doing so, she stood up, untangling all the cords and running all but the red Dancing Channel cable between the two columns of boxes down in front of the television and out of the way. She was beginning to sweat as the television set was positioned very close to the living room's radiator.

"Okay," she said. "Testing every socket on the adaptor." One after another, she plugged the Dancing Channel line-out cable into the ten sockets on the adaptor, quickly turning on and off the knob on the Dancing Channel box each time as the signal came in perfectly each time. "Okay, so it's not the jacks on the adaptor, but it could be . . . what? Oh, right, the Wedding Channel cable. This is getting confusing."

Cinderella unplugged the red cable from the back of the Dancing Channel box and the other red cable from the back of the Wedding Channel box. Inspecting the plug, she couldn't see anything noticeably wrong with it. The Dancing Channel cable still plugged into the tenth socket of the adaptor, she plugged the other end into the line-out socket on the Wedding Channel box. She turned the knob on. Nothing.

She sighed. "Okay, so, the adaptor is fine, and I know this cable is fine, so it could be the jack on the back of the box, but I have no way to test it, so I can at least test the cable running into the box."

Making the Dancing Channel's line-out cable the new Wedding Channel line-out cable, she plugged one end of the old Wedding Channel's cable into the back of the Dancing Channel box and its other end into the adaptor. She then plugged the remaining five cables from the five other boxes into the adaptor. "Okay, that's back to normal," she said. To be sure, she flipped on the Dancing Channel. It worked. "So, it definitely wasn't the Wedding Channel's line-out cable," she said, turning off the Dancing Channel.

Sappho looked up at her, then lowered her head and stretched out on the couch. "I'm dizzy," Cinderella said to Sappho. The dog yawned.

Cinderella looked to the back of the Wedding Channel box. Above the socket from which the line-out cable ran to the adaptor was the socket into which the blue line-in cable running up out of the basement was screwed. The other end of that cable was in the junction box in the dining room. "Okay, need to test this cable," she said. She attempted to unscrew it from the back of the Wedding Channel box, but it had been screwed too tightly to undo with fingers.

"And now I need a wrench," she said to Sappho. The dog looked away, disinterested.

First, however, she went into the dining room to see if she needed a screwdriver to open the junction box that had the seven premium channel cables running out the bottom and into a hole in the floor as she was pretty sure she did. Sure enough, there were two screws she had to undo, but she was surprised upon inspecting their heads and finding a six-pointed star-shaped pattern.

"Seriously?" Cinderella grumbled.

In the corner of the kitchen near the back door was the cable closet. Next to it, below the counter top on which sat Cinderella's coffeemaker, was the tool drawer. Rummaging through this, Cinderella, to her great surprise, found a screwdriver with a six-pointed head, no doubt the exact match in size to the junction box screws. Deciding to forgo testing three of the wrenches to figure out which size matched the tightly screwed plug on the channel box best, after some searching, she grabbed a pair of adjustable pliers.

Finding what she wanted in the cable closet was not to be so easy. Its three walls were covered in hooks from which hung coiled cables of every type. Boxes of tangled cords sat on the floor. From high fidelity stereo component cables and speaker wires, to telephone and modem cords, to electrical extension cords and cleaning and kitchen appliance wires, to television and premium channel cables, and to a variety of cable types whose use remained a mystery to her, the closet held it all. Fortunately, after much hunting, she found it held a fairly lengthy line-in cable for premium channel boxes, purple in color.

Using the pliers, Cinderella unscrewed the cable from the back of the Wedding Channel box and replaced it with the end of the purple cable she had found in the cable closet, tightening it only as tight as it need be by use of her fingers. Running the cable across the living room floor and into the dining room, she quickly discovered the cable was not going to be long enough. She went back to the television set and pushed it as far as she could towards the dining room without having to undo any of the cabling. Back in the dining room, she attempted to unscrew the star-shaped screws but found they were tighter than expected. "Who tightened everything so damn tight around here?" she asked. Putting more muscle into it, she loosened the screws and made quick work with her fingers, leading the screws out of their holes.

Opening the junction box, she felt the warm air rushing out through the hole in the house from which came in the seven premium channel cables. A thick band ran through the center of the box with twenty jacks, ten at the top for cables coming in from the outside, ten at the bottom for the continuation of the signal from those cables into the house. Cinderella sincerely hoped this part of the connection had the cable that had gone bad, and she had a sneaking suspicion it was. At any rate, she had no desire to follow the cables outside into the cold.

"Too many cables," Cinderella said.

She decided to test from right to left. However, she quickly realized the adjustable pliers were too large to unscrew the overly-tightened cables in the box, and she went back into the kitchen and gathered a few wrenches. The third of three fitted perfectly, and she untightened the rightmost bottom cable, disconnecting it with her twirling fingers. She screwed in the purple cable, then stood up and walked into the living room, realizing it was getting late and that she should probably eat something. Standing before the television set, her mind now focused on her aching lower back, she flipped on the Wedding Channel box, but nothing came in. Leaving it on, she went back to the junction box, unscrewed the purple cable, reattached the blue cable, untightened and unscrewed the next blue cable, and screwed the purple cable into that jack. Nothing. She was getting frustrated. She was hungry, tired, and sore. It was her Birthday. It was Sigillaria. She thought of her stepsisters and stepmother at the Ball, and she grew angry. One after another she tried the jacks. Nothing each time until the seventh, the first from the left. From the living room she heard wedding music.

She stood up, elated. "That solves that!" she laughed. She walked into the living room. On the television was a show about wedding etiquette. She stuck her finger in her mouth, making a puke gesture. "Thank God!" she exclaimed, and by God she meant Gravity, the Creator and Destroyer of All Things, or so she had been taught.

The doorbell rang. Turning around, Cinderella opened the door to be met by five carolers, blurred through the sheet of ice on the glass and metal outer door, who immediately burst into song. This dampened her spirits. She had repeatedly told her stepmother the door frame needed rebuilt and had been using spray foam insulation as an ongoing, temporary solution. She wasn't sure they had any left. Cinderella shook her head. "I don't have any money to give you," she said and closed the door.

Turning back around, she headed for the kitchen to see if they had a can of spray foam insulation and immediately tripped on the taut purple cable. The Wedding Channel box spun off the television set and on to the floor, the station cutting out. The Dancing Channel box fell behind the television. Sappho jumped off the couch and ran to the Wedding Channel box. She sniffed it.

"Shit!" Cinderella exclaimed.

The line-out cable had been pulled out as the box had fallen, but by the angle the purple line-in cable was protruding from the box as she picked it up off the floor, she knew there was a problem. Sure enough, the plastic was cracked, and the jack was torn out from the box at a ninety-degree angle.

"Well, now it's the jack," she said, sighing and setting the box down on the floor. Sappho sniffed it again and walked into the kitchen.

Behind the television set, Cinderella found the Dancing Channel box undamaged, its fall broken by a bed of cables. She turned off the television. Sitting on the floor, she inspected the torn jack of the Wedding Channel box. The socket had ripped from the circuit board to which it was attached. As she attempted to unscrew the cable, the remaining plastic cracked. She knew nothing of circuitry and soldering, but she knew all about replacing hardware, having built and rebuilt her personal computer since she could remember. Looking at the box, she found it was a simple matter of unscrewing four star-shaped screws to get into it. Taking the box into the dining room and sitting down at the table, she used the star-shaped screwdriver to get into it. The socket of the jack had been ripped from the box, and there was no chance of replacing it alone, but slid into a long, thin socket inside the box was the removable Wedding Channel card. If she could get a new box, she could swap the card into that one. Leaving the box on the table, she gathered up the purple premium channel cable.

In the kitchen, Sappho was sleeping in her pet bed by the stove. Cinderella grabbed the phonebook off the top of the refrigerator and flipped through the thin paper of its pages until she found the listing for Kate's Electronics, the little store at which she often window-shopped on Mireille Street. Grabbing the phone off its hook on the wall and holding it with her left hand at her waist as the dial tone blared, she used the index finger of her right hand to enter in the seven digit number on the rotary dial. After a few seconds, she heard the cadence of the ring and held up the handset as the Kate's Electronics employee at the other end picked up.

"Hello?" she asked. "We're closing."

Cinderella looked at her watch. "What? Why are you closing now?" she asked in disbelief.

"Um, the holiday," the clerk said.

"Oh. Never mind then," said Cinderella. She hung up the phone.

Her only other option then was Turms, a big box store that she hated, but they carried everything and were closed for nothing. She flipped through the phonebook and found the listing for the one on Kirika Avenue, closest to her. She dialed the number.

"Turms Customer Service," said a raspy woman's voice.

"Could I have Electronics, please?" Cinderella asked politely.

"Please hold," the voice grated.

Music emitted from the earpiece, an instrumental rendition of a Sigillaria tune Cinderella recognized but didn't. Bored, she began to twirl herself in the lengthy phone cord.

"Did you have to take a cigarette break first?" Cinderella asked into the receiver.

"Electronics," a teenager's voice cracked. Cinderella assumed it was male.

"Hello," Cinderella said.

"Can I help you?" the pubescent boy asked.

"Yes, do you carry premium channel boxes?" Cinderella asked.

"The subscription plans?" the clerk asked. "Or do you mean the replacement boxes?"

"The replacement boxes," Cinderella said.

"Yes, we carry those," the clerk said. "They might not look like your current box, but they accept the cards all the same. They come with all the channel stickers you can affix."

"That's good," said Cinderella.

"You'll need a special, star-shaped screwdriver to get the boxes open though," the clerk added.

"Yes, I know," said Cinderella. "I have one. Do you have them in stock?"

"The boxes?" the clerk asked. "Or—"

"Yes," said Cinderella.

"The boxes?" the clerk repeated.

"Yes, the boxes," said Cinderella.

"Yes, we have them in stock," the clerk said.

"Another thing," Cinderella said. "Could you check to see if you have any fifty foot," and Cinderella held up the cable to her eyes, trying to read the white numbering on the purple cable, "any fifty foot Alpha Chi Zero Zero Seven Four Eight Four cable?"

She heard a bit of a snicker. "Yes, we do," the clerk said.

"Oh, you do," Cinderella said happily. Then skeptically asked, "Are you sure?"

"Yes," the clerk said. "Anything else I can help you with?"

"No," Cinderella said. She set the coiled, purple cable down beside her coffeemaker. "Oh, wait! Can you hold one of each for me?" she hurriedly asked.

"Sorry, ma'am, we don't hold," the clerk said.

"Oh, um, okay. Bye." She untwirled herself and hung up the receiver. "Ma'am?" she asked. "Do I sound that old?"

Wanting to be done and over with this, she made sure she had turned off the television set in the living room, pushed it back in its place, hastily blew out the candles on the mantle, and turned off all the lamps in the living room but one. Her stepmother and stepsisters stored their outdoor attire in the closet at the front of the house. Cinderella was left with a hook and bench in the kitchen at the back. She removed her bag and boots from the bench, and one after another she tightly tied them against it.

"No," she said to Sappho who had awoken and walked over to her. "We're not going for a walk. I have to go to the store."

She pulled on her long brown coat and threw up the hood. Then she remembered she hadn't checked to see if they had any insulating foam. Searching through the cupboard under the drawer in which she found the screwdriver, she found none.

"You be good," she said, moving past Sappho.

Cinderella opened the door and flipped off the kitchen light. With her bag across her chest, she stepped out the door into the cold, pulling the strings on her hood and slipping on her gloves in the illumination of the back porch light.

Chapter 4

Cinderella hadn't stepped very far down the stone garden path at the back of the house before she felt her boots were too loose. She made her way through the snow to a wrought iron garden bench near the remnants of last season's frost pumpkin patch, took off her gloves, and with her right foot up on the bench and then her left foot, untied and retied each boot. When she stood erect again, the pain in her lower back became more pronounced, and she flinched. "Forget taking a shower tonight," she said as she pulled her gloves back on and returned to the path, "I'm taking a bath."

The shoveled stone path ended at the property line between a detached garage on Cinderella's left and the hazelnut tree planted in memory of her mother on her right. Beneath the tree, two white squirrels on the ground chattered, looking for fallen nuts in the snow. Stopping and gazing at the tree, first at its trunk, then up at the bare branches, Cinderella raised her pressed together middle and index finger to her lips and held them there for four seconds, giving two seconds of silence to each of her dead parents, as was the custom.

No fence closed off the yard, and through a forest of young trees a path of trampled snow continued on to a looping stone path laid down by the city and lit by lampposts. Cinderella followed this path through the park to the trailhead. From there, she took the stone path out of the forest to the sidewalk running along Mireille, a street whose various shops she frequented regularly.

Those shops were closed now, and so she headed up the road to the nearest tram stop, relieved that tram 12 was arriving just as she was, sparks flying from the wires above as it came to a rest and the doors opened. Boarding, she rushed to take a seat, the car quickly filling with mostly young holiday revelers heading out to parties and bars. For a minute, Cinderella was jealous of them, but then became annoyed at their loud, obnoxious behavior, the ones closest to her, students of the local high school, bragging about how they were going to beat up a particular group of students from another school. No elder on the tram challenged their behavior, and so it continued. Cinderella reached into her bag and pulled out her portable audio cassette player. She slipped the earbuds between her hood into her ears and pressed the oval play button on the device. The love theme from the *Fiona in Fairyland: Songs of Sorrow 2* video game filled her ears as the wheels on the cassette player spun and the tram clacked down the tracks.

As much as Cinderella disliked being in the house with her stepmother and stepsisters, she disliked going out into the world more. The first problem was that while she could stand the cold, as every native of Amalthea could stand the cold, she didn't care for it. More importantly, however, Cinderella disliked going out because of the people. People were noisy, people were loud, and you never knew what weird or obnoxious type you were going to encounter. Her stepmother and stepsisters were predictable, and she had found that if she stayed out of their way and did her work and didn't complain about what little financial payment she received in return, they left her alone in the evenings when she retreated to her room in the basement. In the world there was no place to retreat to, and strangers bumped and yelled and generally acted like the world belonged to them when it didn't, it belonged to everyone, and that made Cinderella angry.

Cinderella's only practical skills being cooking

and cleaning, when she had turned eighteen, she had sought housecleaning work in her district but found the women who employed her to have even more unreasonable expectations than her stepmother, as if the King and Queen were coming to their home to dine and defecate. She had also sought out work as a cook but had been turned down at every place she had applied, not on account of her cooking, which no one had even bothered to sample, but on account of her lack of a culinary degree, as if she needed a degree to do something she had done daily since childhood. Enough early incidents such as these had caused her to give up, to not bother, and so she had resigned herself to the fate of maid in her childhood home, a job she had performed most of her life, but which now came with a pittance.

Still, she dreamed of Ophion. She had been saving up the best she could to purchase a train ticket and start a new life there. Daphne, her best friend from high school, had moved there upon graduation and had promised to help her start out, but their correspondence had dropped to being only monthly, then bimonthly, and now for the past five months, Cinderella hadn't even heard back from her.

While Cinderella longed to move to Ophion, much of the rest of Amalthea longed to kick out the immigrants from it. Almost half of the population of Amalthea had been killed in the dragon attack twenty years ago with very little of the city having not been burned down or later demolished. Emerging from the battle victorious, the survivors were quick to rebuild, but not without enormous financial backing and labor coming from Ophion whose leaders realized how dependent they were on the azoth mines on the Rhea Plateau. The people of Amalthea worried that from the bankers to the builders, their culture was being invaded by Ophion. Accusing the monarchy of selling out the city to foreigners, so strong was the paranoia in Amalthea that the Conservative Party had taken seven of the twelve Council seats in the last election. Cinderella could not have cared less. Ophion had given her everything *Fiona in Fairyland*. Amalthea had given her misery, and her goal, no matter now vague it was now, remained to get out.

The pain shot through her stomach and she curled over. Having forgotten to eat again and again, she now had to eat to stem off the pain. She rummaged through her bag for something, but found nothing, as the pain again tore through her stomach. She imagined a cat scratching it from the inside. This wasn't the first time this week she had forgotten to eat, and she grew worried she was becoming absentminded to her own body.

Fortunately, it was only a couple minutes to her stop. Getting off the tram, she rushed into the nearly deserted Istvan's fast-food hamburger restaurant, one of those complained about cultural imports from Ophion. Slipping away her cassette player and pulling out her wallet, she approached the counter.

"Welcome to Istvan's, may I help you?" the teenaged female cashier said.

"Yes, give me a Farmer's Combo with . . . ," Cinderella began, scanning the list of beverages. "Give me a beer, please," she said.

She was in an Istvan's, far from her neighborhood, in an area of town where no one knew her, and she was surprised to find that the cashier did not ask for her identification card to verify her age, the legal drinking age in Amalthea being eighteen. She wondered how old she looked to the cashier as she paid her, reading the sign on the register informing that they card for alcohol anyone who appeared under the age of thirty-five.

Fortunately, her order came up fast. Taking her

tray of food to a seat by the door next to the window, she looked at the clock hanging on the wall, unwrapped her sandwich, and ate and drank hurriedly, not even taking off her coat. Her mind began to wander. Her original plan of the evening to get some gaming in having been dashed, she still planned to get something fun in before bedtime. Maybe an episode of a television show, she thought. She had been wanting to begin rewatching the first series of *Fiona in Fairyland* for some time now. However, first she had to get the cable and premium channel box replaced for her stepfamily so they could continue to spend their evenings watching the Wedding Channel, among all the other pointless premium channels to which they subscribed, filling their already banal lives with thoughts of happily every after, dreaming of marital days spent blissfully redecorating dreadful rooms with additional knickknacks and preparing convoluted menus and centerpieces for dinner parties.

Cinderella began to choke she ate so fast. Slowing down, she tried to savor her food, as it was savory. The burger of her Farmer's Combo was called so because the beef patty was piled on with vegetables of every sort. Some cities built statues to honor the work of their farmers; Ophion romanticized its farmers by naming a fast-food hamburger after them. Cinderella knew, however, that those farmers, quickly being replaced by machination, their farms consumed by the expanding city, and Ophion's general shift towards importing food from its colonies, ate no such thing. They couldn't afford the beef.

Stuffed, she put her fried potato chips into a paper bag she had in her crossbody for such occasions, stowed them away, finished her beer, deposited her garbage in the appropriate recycling bins, tossed up her hood and put on her gloves, and headed out the door.

"What's up, baby?" one of the teenagers from the tram said, entering the restaurant as she exited.

It bothered Cinderella she couldn't go out into the world without being bothered, but having just eaten, she kept a positive mood. Not a lightweight, the beer gave her the buzz she needed to get through the remainder of her shopping trip while not otherwise impairing her ability. However, when she exited the Istvan's, at first she was confused, surprised to see she was across from Turms and not among the shops of her neighborhood. The interior of every Istvan's looked the same, after all.

Cinderella crossed the street at the light, a Philo's fuel station being at the corner on the opposite end. Despite azoth being mined by the city, liquid azoth as an automobile fuel was far more expensive in Amalthea than in other cities on account of Amalthea not having its own liquefaction plant, necessitating the need to import it. While liquid azoth burned clean, the process to liquefy it was not, and the people of Amalthea were not eager to have such a plant in their valley. Cinderella hadn't driven her father's old car since her graduation from high school, yet she naturally looked to see what the price was, finding it higher than normal on account of the holiday travel. While the city had one of the best mass transit systems in the world, those who could afford an automobile avoided it.

Rather than follow the sidewalk, Cinderella cut through the snow. In so doing, she noticed some graffiti on the side of the fuel station. In red letters it read, "Now you have license, slave, to game with your master." Cinderella didn't know what the graffiti meant, but it made her long to be sitting in her basement room in front of her computer.

She cut across the parking lot and entered Turms. The store was built on the location of two former glass factories which had so successfully competed with one another, they had driven themselves bankrupt and were both purchased by a company in Ophion which shut them down, paving the way for the first Turms to be constructed in Amalthea. An elderly greeter did not meet her as she walked past the shopping carts, but she did notice two burly security guards, one of which eyed her suspiciously. The air was dry, the florescent lights blinded her, but, fortunately, the store wasn't crowded.

Cinderella's "get in, get out" attitude dissipated as she looked upon a towering and wide display of toy figures for the holiday flanked on either side by smaller displays of holiday candles, the latter now 75% off. The toys were a motley crew of all the popular franchises of the times, some of them limited edition variations for the holidays. A quick survey of the display revealed there were no *Fiona in Fairyland* figures, not unsurprising to Cinderella since *Fiona in Fairyland* was from her youth and far more popular in Ophion than in Amalthea. When she was four, her father had visited Ophion for some reason or another and had returned with a *Fiona in Fairyland* figure for her fifth birthday. That had begun Cinderella's obsession with the franchise. By comparison, she thought the toys and cartoons of today were trash. Mutant firefighting rats, zombie school children, and guys who dressed up like wombats to combat crime just did not appeal to her now, and she doubted they would have appealed to her as a child. She found a vanilla scented candle on the neighboring display, sniffed it, and smiled.

Recalling why she was at the store, she headed for the Electronics department, the candle in hand, but her attention was quickly grabbed by the myriad magazines on the shelves to her left. Glancing from cover to cover as she walked, she eventually stopped, set down the candle, and picked up a copy of the latest issue of *Geek Out*. She flipped through it searching for any news on anything *Fiona in Fairyland* or any of the other four franchises she still followed from her youth but found nothing. As for the modern franchises and their fandoms in the magazine, Cinderella concluded she just didn't care for them. She used to wonder if it was because she had so little time for franchises and fandoms anymore, but she had grown to understand that geek culture was changing. It wasn't that she had no time to adequately participate, it was that so many geeks these days didn't put what she considered adequate time into their participation. They jumped from book to book, game to game, show to show without ever really putting in the time to learn everything they possibly could about the franchise. Cinderella understood that no one could know everything, but there was a reason an intellectual property ended up a franchise, and for people to know so little about it yet call themselves fans and be called fans by magazines like *Geek Out* was wrong. Desire was an integral part in being a geek. One had to have the desire for more, but also the desire to know more. It mattered to her because in the player versus player combat of *Fairyland Lost*, she frequently found herself teamed up with people not only ignorant of the lore but incompetent at the game complaining about mechanics integral to the franchise and making mistakes from which they refused to learn. When Cinderella had called such so-called gamers poseurs in a chat room once, all hell had broken loose. She tossed the copy of *Geek Out* back onto the magazine rack and headed for Electronics, forgetting the candle.

Cinderella was angry at herself for wasting time on the magazine. She made it a point to overlook everything in Electronics and went straight for the cables. Sure enough, they carried the cables, not only in a variety of lengths, but in a variety of colors and brands as well. Vesta was the only brand she trusted. She decided on a fifty foot one to be on the safe side, although she supposed thirty-five feet would be enough. As for color, she wanted one other than blue. Trying to decide between red and green, she made up her mind it didn't matter, and chose red after a few more seconds wasted deliberating.

Unlike the cables, the premium channel replacement boxes she had to hunt for, but she refused to ask the gangly clerk for assistance as he would no doubt remember the phone call and start up a conversation. The boxes were as generic as they came, but they looked to be what she wanted, and so she grabbed one and moved on to Hardware, cutting through Decor, which she quickly realized was a mistake as everything from the floor lamps and coffee tables to framed prints and statues caught her eye.

She stopped at a shelf on which were displayed various fairies made of porcelain, polyresin, and glass. Cinderella wanted to believe in fairies. She wanted to believe in these tiny, beautiful, gentle winged creatures who could do types of magic of which high sorcerers could only ever dream. She knew there were angels, of course, if the stories of her father and others were to be believed, but they were far from the benign creatures before her. One fairy she took particular interest in was made entirely of glass. Sitting cross-legged on a glass ball wearing a glass dress, the glass fairy had her enormous glass wings spread out behind her. Cinderella admired the detail of the fairy, too afraid to touch it. The craftsmanship was so fine, the detail so precise, the fairy even wore high-heeled slippers of glass. Cinderella found the price of the glass fairy on a listing to her left. She shook her head and continued on.

In Hardware, she quickly found the cans of spray foam insulation, but not recognizing the brands, Cinderella checked each to make sure she had indeed found what she was looking for, thinking she should have just waited until tomorrow and gone to the local hardware store. Finally, she managed to find a can with specifications to her liking. She headed for the cash registers at the front of the store. However, she passed the walled-off Magic department on the way, and since she was now of legal age to enter it unsupervised, she thought she would take a look. The attendant stared at her suspiciously as she entered the section, but he did not confront her with the need to see her identification card.

For the student of magic, Turms carried it all. Amazed at everything she was seeing, Cinderella put her three items in a shopping basket, the attendant looking at them condescendingly, and walked over to a large selection of books for beginners. They were all thick. She set down her basket and picked one up at random. Flipping to the Table of Contents, she read the chapter titles:

1. Anima and Psyche
2. Azoth
3. You and Your Training Orb
4. Gemstones
5. Trinkets, Amulets, and Talismans
6. Your First Rod

Cinderella had heard mention of anima and psyche before, knowing that through them she could feel and work magic, but she had not yet felt it, and she wondered if she would without training. Glancing through Chapter 1 to see if anything grabbed her attention, she found the passages she skimmed dense. She set down the book and moved on.

Both sides of the rest of the aisle were filled with a large selection of training orbs available in a variety of metals, designs, and sizes, the most common being plain silver ones the size of a softball, all of them floating in clear plastic boxes. A plain copper one caught Cinderella's eye. To her surprise, it was pricey. She knew that sooner or later she was going to have to purchase one. Everyone did. She made a mental note to step into her neighborhood magic shop when she went out to the markets tomorrow to see their selection, and she continued down the remainder of the aisles without even registering for the most part what she was seeing. At one aisle's endcap was a container of loose, polished gemstones of every color. She wanted to take off her coat, roll up her sleeves, and dip her arms down into them, but thought otherwise.

The last aisle Cinderella found to be lined with robes of varying colors, fabrics, and sizes with long rectangular tags hanging from them. Curious, Cinderella grabbed one of the tags and found that it was sewn into the inside of the sleeve. At the top, it read, "UNDER PENALTY OF LAW THIS TAG NOT TO BE REMOVED EXCEPT BY THE CONSUMER," followed by the manufacturer of the azoth-treated cotton thread, the names of who applied the magic to the fabric, and a long listing of what Cinderella knew were the statistics of the robe but which she could not read to understand. All magical robes carried various resistances which emitted different auras, often remaining invisible to the untrained, which reduced the effects of the environment and withstood spells constructed from those elements. Popular among the mages of Amalthea were robes which reduced the effects of the chilling cold, while in places such as Kresnik, magicians wore robes which reduced the effects of the heat. Robes had unisex appeal and easily protected the wearer in their auras as the fabric covered almost the whole body. However, custom clothing designed to match the fashions of the day was not unheard of, but stronger magic had to be worked into the material for the auras to fully protect the wearer. While in most cases not designed to withstand magical attacks, the dresses for the Sigillaria Ball were crafted to cloak the wearer in warmth. Cinderella had even heard tales of the sorcerers of Eurynome who hunted kraken in nothing but swimming suits so powerful was the magic in the fabric. As a general rule, the skimpier the clothing, the more powerful the magician, and many unsuspecting attackers throughout the ages had found themselves instead at the mercy of sorcerers wearing what appeared only to be street clothes.

Satisfied she had seen enough, Cinderella left the Magic department and headed towards the cash registers, stopping in the aisle at the squeaking of her name.

"Cinderella! Cinderella!" came the high-pitched voice from behind her.

Cinderella turned around. A well-dressed, well-groomed woman rushed up to her holding a bottle of wine in each hand, one red, one white. Cinderella didn't recognize her at first but then realized it was Selene, a friend of Daphne. The last time Cinderella had seen Selene, her hair was purple and she had piercings. Looking at Selene's obsessively made-up face, Cinderella detected a scar on her perfectly plucked left eyebrow.

"How are you?" Selene squeaked. "How excited were you when you heard about the engagement?"

"I'm fine," Cinderella muttered. "What engagement?" Her head swirled.

"Daphne's engagement!" Selene shouted.

Cinderella flinched. "Daphne is engaged?" she asked. "To be married?"

"You mean you didn't know?" Selene asked.

"No," Cinderella said.

"Oh my God!" Selene said, her jaw jutting and her eyes bugging. "Well, now you do. I'm so excited for her. I'm still waiting for Endymion to ask me." She laughed. "Me and him are going to Daphne's place in Ophion for New Year's. It's gonna be so fun. What are you doing?"

"Now?" Cinderella asked.

"No, for New Year's," Selene said.

"I haven't thought about it yet," Cinderella said.

"Oh. Well, hate to keep you. Gotta run. Good seeing you again," Selene said and rushed off for the cash registers, her heels clattering.

Cinderella found her mood to now be foul. She stood there in the aisle, warm, staring blankly at a candy cane display. After a minute, she looked up and saw the Shoe department sign hanging from the rafters. Having already wasted enough time in the store, she did not hesitate to head for it. Cinderella knew she didn't need new shoes, but she needed something for herself for her birthday and Sigillaria. The glass fairy statue would be nice to have, but it was a luxury item and too expensive. A magic training orb she would need to buy if she was going to attempt to learn magic, but at this point it was nothing more than an overly expensive school supply in a discipline she was not yet ready to enter. She could head over to Toys and see what they had, but she didn't want something the primary purpose of which was that of a child's toy. She was a maid. For recreation, she played video games, and her interests were often those of a child. Yet, tonight, she wanted to feel feminine, and it was high-heeled shoes and the gait-enhancing femininity they granted to which she gravitated. They were also always on sale.

The decade following the victory over the dragons had been a liberal-minded decade, and while the high heel was never wont to go out of fashion, the heels of that decade had been thick and blocky. However, the past ten years had seen a resurgence of clearly-defined gender and class roles brought about by the conservative, cultural paranoia surrounding the issue of the Ophion immigrants in Amalthea who refused to leave after the rebuilding of the city, and, as a consequence, the plain, pointed-toe box stiletto heel had come back into fashion. Likewise, Ophion had grown more conservative as well, its people questioning the outpouring of foreign aid to Amalthea.

But the times were changing. The world over was becoming more bold, and the shoes on display before Cinderella were like nothing she had ever seen. The stiletto remained, but it had increased in height on account of the platform toe box which had additionally become rounded and open. The vamp was high and the back zippered and the shoes were not leather but satin with a thick ankle strap.

"Peep-Toe Ankle Strap Platforms," Cinderella read off the box in amazement of a teal pair her size. She didn't recognize the brand. "Designed and Made in Eurynome."

Centuries ago, before the rise of Ophion, Eurynome had been the most powerful and influential city on Terra. With such a difference in design when it came to the age-old high heel, Cinderella wondered what else its people were up to.

Sitting on a bench, she took off her boots and socks, rolled up the end of her leggings, and was quick to try on the heels. Though high, they offered much in the way of support for the foot, and the padding was abundant. She walked back and forth, watching herself in the scattered mirrors. The last she had worn heels was at high school graduation, but she quickly adjusted to them. Ten years of dance and ballet lessons hadn't been for naught on her. Walking off the carpet, she tested the shoes on the hard floor of the aisle. Satisfied, she reboxed them and headed for the cashiers.

As she had only four items, Cinderella chose a self-checkout lane. The three items for the house she scanned and bagged first and then paid for them with her stepmother's credit card she had been authorized to use, feeding the card into a reader above the scanner, signing with an ink pen on a cord a receipt which printed out, and then feeding that receipt back into the machine before her copy of the receipt printed out and the card was ejected. She hesitated before scanning the shoes. They weren't something she needed, and she had just enough cash for them. She stood there realizing just how tired and sore she was from the day's work, and with that she grabbed the box, scanned and bagged it, fed in the money, collected her change and receipt, and headed for the exit. There, she set her bags in an abandoned shopping cart before bundling up for the cold. She had to use the restroom, but not wanting to use a public one, she decided to wait until she got home. The beer, she thought, might not have been the best idea.

Outside, the sky was clear and the temperature had dropped. Cinderella had spent her whole life in Amalthea and was certain it would soon be snowing. She hurriedly made her way to the tram stop, finding to her displeasure the youths from the earlier tram and Istvan's there. She moved farther down the platform away from them.

One approached her, the same that had bothered her before.

"Hey, missus, you got any change for a telephone call?" he asked.

Cinderella didn't say anything.

"You got a boyfriend, lady?" the boy said, grabbing his groin. The other boys with him giggled.

She ignored him, transferring the shopping bag with the shoe box from her right hand to her left and unzipping her crossbody.

"You whore," the boy said, standing five feet away from her.

Cinderella reached into her bag and clutched her switchblade, shaking. Her father had been a soldier. She had been trained to defend herself should the need arise.

The boy turned and walked away from her, but Cinderella did not loosen her grip on the knife until the tram arrived. She waited until the boys boarded the second car, then rushed back up the platform to the first car, boarding it just as the doors closed.

She stumbled as the tram headed off, clutching a pole until a seat opened up at the next stop.

As the tram traveled through the darkness sparingly lit by city lights, Cinderella stared out the window, catching glimpses of closed storefronts and the occasional pedestrian, noticing after some time the tram window was rattling in its metal frame. It didn't bother her. Yet, she felt the need to correct it. Barely realizing what she was doing, she turned to the window and raised her left hand as if to press against the glass. But she did not. She held it inches away. Though her hand was gloved and she was not touching the window, she could feel the cold of the glass. The rattling had stopped. Shocked, she withdrew her hand and the rattling resumed, the window banging as the tram slowed down to make her stop.

Cinderella did not dwell. Stepping off the tram, she found the temperature had only continued to drop, and so she rushed, nearly running, up the street and through the park. Upon reaching the back door of the house, she mistyped the keycode on account of her gloved hand. Pulling off the glove, she quickly typed in the keycode again. The door unlocked. Cinderella stepped into the warm house, relieved to be closing the door on the cold.

She hung up her coat, put away her boots, and set her bag and the shopping bag with the shoes on the kitchen table. In the living room, she set the other shopping bag next to the television set before sinking into an armchair, exhausted.

Chapter 5

When Cinderella awoke, she wasn't sure the time or the place, but then she recognized the living room from the glow of the kitchen, and turning to the television set, she saw the Turms bag. Sappho was asleep at her feet. Cinderella looked to the grandfather clock beside the lamp before the window. It was just after nine.

"Crap," she said. She nudged Sappho with her foot. The dog awoke and walked into the kitchen. Cinderella stood, her lower back cracking. As the pain in her back increased with each movement, she felt she desperately needed some relief and comfort. First, however, she needed to use the bathroom. She hurriedly went into the ground floor bathroom which always smelled strongly of cleaning chemicals. She sneezed thrice as she sat down on the toilet.

Cinderella had planned to take a bath and get something fun in tonight, but making her way into the kitchen she figured she'd just take a quick shower, get in an arena match in *Fairyland Lost*, and head to bed. She let Sappho outside, watching her through the door's window for a moment before closing her eyes and resting her head against the glass. Quick about her business in the cold, Sappho pawed the door to be let back in. Cinderella yawned. The cable and premium channel box would have to wait until tomorrow, but as she would no doubt be the first one up, and as her stepmother was unlikely to care to notice anything when they arrived home from the Ball, Cinderella figured it could safely wait until morning. However, she did retrieve her cleaning supplies from the living room, remembering her stepmother's orders to have the fire burning when they arrived home as she picked her dropped rag off the floor. She would have to remember to set her alarm on her computer. Cinderella grabbed her crossbody and shopping bag off the table, flipped off the light switch to the kitchen, and headed into the dark basement, flipping on a switch at the bottom of the steps.

Though not a finished basement, two radiators had been installed, keeping the room warm, and Cinderella had crafted a portion of it into comforting, livable space. The wall at the bottom of the stairs was bare except for a radiator while against the wall beside the stairwell sat the washer and dryer, the clothesline from which today's laundry hung hiding them from view. Two bookshelves piled with paperback novels, comic books, audiotapes, videotapes, and video game cartridges stood opposite the radiator wall, a radiator fixed to it as well. Opposite the washer and dryer was Cinderella's bathroom built into the corner, her wardrobe next to it. Beside it in the corner was the fuse cabinet. Her bed sat in the open on a square of the old living room carpet, and lining its foot and the side along the bookshelves was her desk: two rectangular folding tables placed perpendicularly to each other, enough space to walk between them and her bed, between them and her bookshelves. On this piece of unsophisticated furniture sat every matter of modern electronic device, their cords not trailing across the floor but rather up to power sockets Cinderella had rigged on the wooden rafters, the excess cabling coiled and hanging from nails while across the ceiling stretched a web of wiring and plumbing. Most of Cinderella's possessions, from the furniture, to her clothing, to the electronics, to the books and video games, had been gifts in her youth or purchased secondhand.

Cinderella tossed the shopping bag with the shoes on her unmade bed and sat her crossbody on her desk by the printer, unfastening her watch and laying it there as well. She looked to her broken PDA atop the printer, the screen smashed and its terminal cord wrapped around it, unable to retract. She had been indecisive on whether to get it fixed or buy a new one, and she began to regret spending the money on the shoes. Next to the printer was her desktop computer, which she turned on, leaving her secondary monitor sitting atop it off. Four orange Network cables ran down from the ceiling and into the back of the desktop. Until two years ago, she had been without Network access, her stepfamily not wanting anything to do with the Information Superhighway, content to get the news and entertainment they craved from television. Cinderella had just wanted Network access to play online games, and the service had been added to her stepmother's home communications package with Cinderella footing the bill for it. She turned on her main monitor and took off her dress, lines of code streaming across the screen as the computer went through its boot cycle. Unfastening her bra, she let out a sigh of relief. She headed to the bathroom in her leggings and socks.

She longed for these moments of the day when she had time to herself in her basement room, and could bathe, and read, and play video games. Today, however, the evening had gone to waste on account of everything to do with the premium channel box, and rather than take a long, hot bubble bath with a good book by candlelight and the scent of vanilla on the air, she was going to have to settle for a quick shower.

She leaned over the bathtub and switched on the rectangular hot water heater hanging on the shower wall, pipes, cables and ducts running into and out of it. Turning on the bathtub faucet, she tested the water before adjusting the temperature dial on the heater. The water was cold, and it was going to take a whole lot of heat to warm it up. Waiting, she inspected the wrinkles around her eyes in the mirror, thinking she should have perhaps spent the money on a good cream instead of on the shoes, and then sat on the toilet and peed. Testing the water again from her seat, she found the temperature acceptable. She stood and pulled a lever up and out on the side of the tub, cutting off the water to the faucet and sending it to the showerhead. Cinderella took off the rest of her clothes and stepped into the shower, drawing the plastic curtain on its cord behind her.

The water was warm, not yet hot, and she longed to take a bath all the more as she rapidly scrubbed herself with vanilla-scented body wash on a mesh sponge. Her short hair she washed quickly, the shampoo vanilla-scented as well. Then she stood there, letting the water cascade off her body as it continued to increase in temperature. She rested her head against the shower wall between the looped hose and let the warm water fall on and down her back. The day had been long. She needed a peaceful rest tonight.

Out of the shower, Cinderella dried herself with her old, worn towel. She slipped on her broken sandals, combed her hair, and walked out into her room, turning on a space heater under her desk. She sat on her bed and let her sandals slip off, replacing them with the high heels she had bought at Turms. She loved their design, but as she had no social reason to wear them, she grew depressed. She thought about returning them, as they were virtually unworn, but she stopped herself when she made to unzip the right one, deciding to live with the purchase and enjoy the shoes how she could. She stood up and began to pace, first on the carpet between her bed and the desk, then on the concrete between the back of her desk and her shelves, eating the leftover fries from her bag and drinking from an opened water bottle she had on her desk as she did so.

She had no full length mirror to see herself in, but she knew the shoes looked good, she knew she looked good in them, and she knew she looked good. She liked the feeling the shoes gave her, but that feeling soon triggered remembrance of her station in life and her misfortune. She realized that these down thoughts were coming about because she was tired, that she needed to get to bed, but she wanted to get one *Fairyland Lost* arena game in before she ended the day. She was good at the game, and victory always lifted her spirits.

Walking to her wardrobe, she found a pair of clean underpants. Without taking off the heels, she stepped into them, checking her balance, which was impeccably good and pleasing to her. Her thoughts now drifting to the Sigillaria Ball, she checked them and pulled on her fleece nightgown. The fabric comforted her.

The *Fairyland Lost* cartridge was still plugged into its console. In fact, it had hardly been removed for two years. She pushed in the power button and turned to her computer monitor, but the screen remained vacant except for the flashing cursor in the upper left. Remembering she had disconnected the console from the port on her desktop and connected her tape deck in its place the previous night, she walked behind her desk and swapped plugs. In doing so, she heard the familiar theme music start up. Returning, she sat in her chair, pointed her mouse cursor at "CONNECT," and clicked. The modem began to beep, whistle and hiss over the *Fairyland Lost* theme music. Then the screeching began. Cinderella hoped it wouldn't take a full five minutes to connect like last night.

She spun around in her chair and kicked up her feet on her bed, admiring the heels as the modem screeched. After some time, she became aware that she was not alone, that something had joined her in the basement, but that it was no living being. She felt cold. Goose bumps broke out on her skin. She pulled a blanket off her bed over her and turned in her chair to face the stairs.

Near the bottom, in the darkness, a dark figure sat. It rose, walking into the light. Its long black robe brushed the concrete floor. The figure folded its black-gloved hands at its midriff as it approached her. She could see nothing of its face. The robe's cowl was pulled low, but Cinderella wasn't sure there was any face beneath that cowl. All that she could define of it was darkness. The figure stopped, standing on the concrete, at the edge of the carpet. When it spoke, Cinderella wasn't convinced the voice she heard came from the body before her, if indeed there was even a body under that robe. Rather, it seemed the voice came from a far off place, as if the figure before her was merely an avatar of something much greater.

"You're not afraid of me?" the figure asked.

Cinderella wasn't sure if it was a question or a statement, nor did she quite fathom that a normal person would naturally be afraid of the figure in black, but that she, naturally, was not.

"No," Cinderella said. Becoming aware of the still-screeching modem, she canceled the connection attempt, taking her eyes off the figure as she did so. Her gaze returning to the figure, she said, "My father told me about you. He said you might show up someday for me. He said our family is cursed."

"No, your family is not cursed," the figure in black said.

"What are you anyway?" Cinderella asked. "My father said you were an angel."

"I am Thanatos. I am Death."

"What exactly does that mean?" Cinderella asked.

"I am all that ever was," Thanatos said.

Cinderella didn't feel that that properly answered the question, but being kind, she did not press Thanatos further. The figure wasn't human, after all. Maybe it didn't understand, she thought.

"Have you come to kill me?" she asked.

"No," said Thanatos.

Cinderella relaxed, only then realizing how tense she actually was. She had not met Thanatos with fear, but her body had gone taut with the angel's sudden appearance.

"Well then, would you like some tea?" Cinderella asked. "You've come unannounced, but I assume that's your way. Otherwise, I would have had the tea made."

"Why do you not fear me?" Thanatos asked.

"Well, you're not going to kill me," Cinderella said. "What's there to fear then?"

"There are worse fates than death," Thanatos said.

"I know," Cinderella said.

"I could, for instance, cripple you," Thanatos said.

"Then I could collect disability and wouldn't

have to work for my stepmother," Cinderella said. "I'd consider that an improvement. But I don't think that's your way. Would you like some tea?" she asked again.

"No, thank you," Thanatos said.

"Well, I'm having tea," Cinderella said, throwing off the blanket.

Though Cinderella had a vivid imagination, when she awoke in the morning to make breakfast for her stepfamily, she couldn't possibly have imagined she would that evening be making tea in high heels in her basement bedroom to drink over conversation with the Angel of Death. She took the kettle from its base on her desk into the bathroom where she filled it up with water, then returned it to its base, flipping on the switch.

"Would you care to have a seat?" Cinderella asked, motioning to her chair. "I can sit on my bed."

"I am fine," Thanatos said.

"Is there anything I can get you?" Cinderella asked. "I'm out of cookies, though," she said, remembering she had forgotten to pick them up when she had gone out shopping both times that day. "Although, I doubt you'd want any."

"No, I am fine," Thanatos said.

Cinderella nodded at the expected answer. As the water began to boil, she grew angry. She was trying to be hospitable with Thanatos. "I'm sorry," she said, "I don't know what to offer you."

"I am fine, Cinderella," Thanatos said.

"And I'm not even sure why I'm trying to be kind to you," she said, throwing her tea bag in her unclean mug and turning to Thanatos, restraining herself from saying anything else.

"What do you mean?" Thanatos asked.

Cinderella said nothing for a moment, but her anger was boiling. "You killed my mother!" she shouted at Thanatos.

"Naturally, you would blame me," Thanatos said.

"'Naturally,'" Cinderella mocked, "you're to blame!"

She turned away from Thanatos and poured water from the kettle into her mug, shaking.

"It was not I who fated your mother to die but your father," Thanatos said. "Nor was it I who delivered your mother but fire rained down upon your family's home by the dragon Nemesis."

"My father said he could have saved my mother, but that you intervened," Cinderella said.

"No one could have saved your mother," Thanatos said. "But, yes, I did intervene, Cinderella.

Did your father ever tell you of our agreement?"

"No." Cinderella paused, remembering. "Well, something, once when he was drunk," she said. "Something that he would have been the one dead and not my mother if not for you."

"Your father and I had an agreement that when his time came another would die in his place," Thanatos said.

"Why?" Cinderella asked.

"Why what?" Thanatos asked.

"Why did you have that agreement?" Cinderella asked. "Do you make that with everybody? Because I'll make an agreement with you now that any member of my stepfamily can die in my place."

"Be careful what you wish for, dear Cinderella," Thanatos said.

Cinderella had heard that expression thrown around many times before, but hearing it now from Thanatos, she gave it heed, nodding. Remembering her tea, she used the tea bag on its string to give it a stir, then tossed the bag in the garbage can at her desk. She took a sip of the hot tea and sat down in her chair.

"Why did you and my father have an agreement?" Cinderella asked, looking to Thanatos.

"When your father was at the Academy, he

found something I had lost," Thanatos said. "For its return, he demanded that I grant him a wish."

"Uh-oh," Cinderella murmured.

"Your father greatly feared a young death, and the recent killing of a young cadet in a training exercise was on his mind," Thanatos said. "Furthermore, he had no love of his parents, having joined the Academy to get away from them. And so the bargain that we struck was this: when his time came, a member of his family would die in his place."

"My grandparents were all dead before my parents married," Cinderella said.

"Exactly," Thanatos said. "Your father was not to die at the Academy, and as time went on, and his parents passed, he forgot about our agreement. He married. Your mother became pregnant. And then the dragons attacked Amalthea."

Cinderella took a sip of her tea.

"The dragon king Predator killed your father," Thanatos began, "but I, honoring our agreement, spared him. His parents dead, your mother had been fated to die in your father's place, and so she did in Nemesis's fire.

"But—" Thanatos stopped.

"'But' what?" Cinderella asked.

"Your mother died wrongfully in place of your father, Cinderella," Thanatos said. "Though as we are aware, no one can escape me, and in time your father came to me."

"I found him, you know, hanging from the hazelnut tree we planted in memory of my mother," Cinderella said.

"Your mother was doomed to die an early death, but you, Cinderella," Thanatos said, approaching her, "I could not take. I saved your life, Cinderella."

Cinderella was not sure of Thanatos's intentions. "What is it you want?" she asked.

"Nothing," said Thanatos, stopping before her.

Cinderella recoiled at the word. The response did not comfort her. She backed away in her chair.

"But that is not what you want," Thanatos said.

Cinderella stared into the abyss beneath the cowl.

"You want to go to Ball," said Thanatos. "I can give you that."

Cinderella looked Thanatos over. There was no way the rangy angel was concealing a dress for the Ball beneath its robe, and she was not sure how benign the supernatural wish granter in front of her was.

"You gonna conjure me a dress?" Cinderella

asked incredulously.

"Something like that," Thanatos said.

"What's the catch?" Cinderella asked.

"Only that this magic will not last long," Thanatos said. "Your purpose in going to the Ball is to commune with the Orb, not to mingle, not to dance."

"What's the fun in going to the Ball if you're not going to dance?" Cinderella asked.

"You will not have the time, Cinderella," Thanatos said.

"Well then," Cinderella said. "What are we waiting for? You have a mask and dress for me?"

"And shoes," Thanatos said.

"What's wrong with these?" Cinderella asked, kicking her feet up in the air as she sat in her chair.

"Would you not prefer something more comfortable?" Thanatos asked.

"I'd prefer glass slippers if you could conjure up a pair of those," Cinderella said.

"Do not be ridiculous," Thanatos replied. "Stand up and take off your nightgown, please."

"You a boy or a girl?" Cinderella asked.

"I am without sex," Thanatos said.

Cinderella stood up and pulled off her nightgown, standing before Thanatos in nothing but underpants and high heels. She instinctively crossed her hands over her breasts.

"This magic will work until midnight," Thanatos said, unfolding its gloved hands and reaching beneath its cowl with its right one, pulling forth a black masquerade mask, its ribbons dangling. The angel handed it to Cinderella.

Cinderella gently took the mask. With the mask against her face, she pulled the black ribbons tight and tied them. Streams of black smoke poured from the mask and circled her body, taking the shape of a black gown. Short in front, long in back, the asymmetrical dress shown off her legs. Looking over the gown she now wore, Cinderella was vaguely aware that the design of the dress, though not the color, was from her own imagination. The lustrous material was alien to her.

"How do I look?" she asked.

"How do you feel?" Thanatos asked in response.

"Wonderful," Cinderella said. She laughed. "How will I get there?" she asked as she walked for the stairs.

"You will drive," Thanatos said behind her as she ascended.

"Drive?" Cinderella asked in the kitchen, reaching for her coat.

"You will not need your coat," Thanatos said.

Sappho in her bed looked up at Cinderella, then to Thanatos, then yawned and set her head back down. She followed them with her eyes as they moved about the kitchen.

"Um, do you know how cold it is out?" Cinderella asked.

"The magic of the dress will keep you warm," Thanatos said.

"Oh, right," Cinderella said. "How am I going to drive?"

"You will take your father's car," Thanatos said, opening the back door.

"My father's car?" Cinderella asked. "It hasn't started in over a year."

"It'll start now," Thanatos said, stepping into the night.

Cinderella was aware that she was not chilled by the heat escaping the house through the open door. Stepping outside, the cold could not touch her. She felt comfortable, as if in a well-heated house.

Thanatos crossed the yard to the garage in the snow. In high heels, Cinderella instead made her way down the sidewalk to the driveway, a light layer of snow covering the concrete, flurries still falling. Normally, she would think that she would have to shovel tomorrow, but no such thought came to her now. Instead, another came to mind.

"When will I die?" she asked Thanatos, stopping.

The angel stopped and turned to her but said nothing. Cinderella repeated the question.

"It isn't written yet," Thanatos said.

"What does that mean?" Cinderella asked.

"It means you nor anyone nor anything have yet determined your fate," Thanatos said. "You could die tomorrow, you could die ten years from now. You will die, but it isn't written yet."

Thanatos turned. The garage door raised itself as the angel approached it.

"I guess that's good news then?" Cinderella asked.

Thanatos said nothing for a moment, then said, "It's pretty remarkable, knowing what I know."

"What is it that you know?" Cinderella asked.

Thanatos did not reply, then said, "Promise me you will commune with the Orb."

"I promise," Cinderella said.

Thanatos turned and stepped into the garage, the fluorescent lights switching on, the flickering glow illuminating the faded red paint of the old, broken-down, two-door car. Her attention drawn to the car, Cinderella almost expected it to start up and the headlights come on as she approached, but it sat there, lifeless.

"You sure it'll start?" Cinderella asked as she passed the angel. "I'm not sure what went wrong with it," she said, getting in, the door unlocked. She noted to her surprise a heavy, brown blanket on the backseat she thought lost. "But it's been sitting so long now I imagine everything is wrong with it."

"It will start," Thanatos said.

Cinderella turned the switch on the center of the dashboard. To her astonishment, the screen above it flickered on, reading "ENTER PASSCODE."

"Well, I'll be damned," she said. "Battery works."

She punched in the seven-digit passcode on the keypad beneath the switch. An asterisk appeared on the screen for each number. She hesitated before pushing the blue power button to the right of the switch, remembering all the times she had made it this far in the startup only to have the engine not respond with the push of the button. She pressed it.

The engine roared to life. The fuel tank read full. "Unbelievable," she said. She rolled down the window. "I don't believe it," she said to Thanatos as she flipped on the headlights. "Now let's see if I can remember how to drive."

She put the car in gear and gently applied pressure to the fuel pedal. The car slowly rolled into the driveway.

"Fasten your seatbelt," Thanatos said.

Cinderella laughed, putting the car into park. She pulled the seatbelt across her and connected it, being careful not to pinch the dress. It dawning on her that she was actually going to the Ball, she became self-conscious, thinking she had not done her hair or applied any makeup. Cinderella flipped down the sun visor. Lights switched on framing a mirror on the backside of it. She looked at her masked visage in it, surprised to see her hair slicked back and side-parted. Likewise, she saw she wore gray eye shadow, eyeliner, and bright red lipstick. She didn't care for the lipstick, and leaned her head out the window. "Can you lighten up the lipstick a bit?" she asked.

Thanatos raised its right hand, its fingers curled and thumb outstretched. The angel pressed its thumb against her lips, then withdrew it. Cinderella thought it was an odd gesture, but when she looked again in the mirror, her lips had lightened.

"Thank you," she said. "Hair is okay, right?"

"You're wasting time," Thanatos said.

"Right," Cinderella said, rolling up the window.

"Be home by midnight," Thanatos said.

Cinderella nodded behind the glass. She put the car in gear and accelerated down the driveway to the street.

Chapter 6

Cinderella drove down the streets of Amalthea towards the Palace as the snow fell. Like wearing high heels, she hadn't driven since high school graduation, but she quickly adjusted as one so easily does to a skill learnt previously. When she stopped at her first stoplight, she instinctively made to remove the masquerade mask to see better, but quickly realizing she was unsure whether doing so would undo Thanatos's magic, she returned her hands to the wheel. The heater she had left off on account of the warmth of the dress, but after a while Cinderella noticed she hadn't even had need to turn on the window defroster. Truly there was magic all around her, she thought.

The layout of Amalthea was simple, and with few cars on the road because of the holiday hour, Cinderella made good time. Just south of the City Center, the lights in the many modest skyscrapers left on for the holiday, she crossed the frozen Undine River from west to east on the Mokosh

Bridge, a cable-stayed bridge named after Amalthea's most famous poet, a contemporary of Capricornus who had published an epic poem about her on the twentieth anniversary of her death. Though not the first to suggest a connection among Capricornus, the Orb, and Static, the popularity of the poem forced the authorities to look into such a connection, with the most learned magical engineers of the time determining that, though the exact nature and magical composition of the Orb remained a mystery, its magical properties were nothing more than that of a glorified training orb. Indeed, the design of training orbs in use today had come about from an attempt to mimic the much larger Orb, but any magical engineer could confidently point out that the magic behind a training orb was well understood and that the magic between a training orb and the Orb of Capricornus was anything but similar. Every few generations, interest was renewed in the Orb, and every time it was studied the conclusions were the same as those of the first engineers to study it. By Cinderella's time, Static was a part of life and civilization, having become something that, on account of its normalcy, was no longer sought to be eradicated, and any attempt to study and somehow link the Orb to Static was considered a complete waste of time.

At Remembrance Plaza, a monument to the fallen of twenty years ago standing at the base of Amalthea's tallest structure, the tower at the top of which was constructed the central node of the Shield's dome, Cinderella turned south, sliding slightly on the snow-covered road. She passed by the power plant on her right and the central television and telephone buildings on her left, cables streaming across the sky every which way, and entered the city's southern district, Amalthea's Old Town, through which the cables from Ophion cut across alongside the well-worn road. Before the dragon attack twenty years ago, many historic buildings, from residential to commercial to industrial, could be found here, some going back to the times surrounding the Revolution when the chief export of the city was quartz and not azoth. Now, the area had been rebuilt, but the building code remained the same in that no structure could be over three storeys high. Near the end of this district was Ianus Hill, on which stood the Royal Palace, Iana Tower, and the rebuilt Ianus Cathedral, Amalthea's oldest remaining structure. Beyond the Hill were the vast Royal Gardens and then

Southgate Fortress where the road and railroad led out of the city and the cables from Ophion came in on the bridge at Perrault Falls.

Cinderella had visited the zoo in the eastern side of the Royal Gardens once as a girl, but she had never been to Southgate and down the bridge and out of the city, just as she had never been up and out of the city at Northwall. Her entire life had been bound by Amalthea's valley walls, but her imagination, aided by books and her computer, had taken her all around the world, and now she was driving up the road cut into the northern face of Ianus Hill on Sigillaria to commune with the Orb where her magical capacity and imagination would be tested.

Many magic teachers knew that a student's failure to advance in magic studies came not from a lack of capability, as all humans were capable, but from a lack of imagination, from an unwillingness or inability to envision a world beyond the one in front of them. The earliest magicians advanced the art much as their minds were open to the possibilities before them and not restricted by the routine of their accomplishments as the generations that followed were. Some foolishly argued in Cinderella's time that everything to know

105

about magic was already known, but the wisest knew there was much magic still to be discovered, that there was much magic that had been worked that was not fully understood, and when some among them argued that age-old restrictions on practices and practitioners should be relaxed, they also knew that not all minds envisioned a better world.

At the top of the Hill, Cinderella drove through the stone walls protecting the grounds at the gate, the guard barely looking up from his desk in his booth. Had she been suspicious, had she posed a threat in any way, the magical sensors would have been triggered on the drive up the Hill. Inside the walls, the road circled around, the roadway lined on either side with upscale vehicles, and as Cinderella passed the conservatory and greenhouse and neared the valet parking attendants in front of the Palace, she became embarrassed, thinking she had no business being on the Hill in such an old and dumpy car.

An attendant approached the curb. Cinderella kept driving, imagining the attendants laughing at her. She passed the Cathedral, the Tower, then the barracks, exiting the grounds at the gate, wondering as she drove down the Hill if she was now considered suspicious. She should have arrived by taxi like everyone else her class, she thought. She started to grow paranoid, thinking that this was all a joke Thanatos was playing on her, that the angel was really a demented little jester trying to get her to look like a fool in front of the upper class. She considered driving home.

Instead, Cinderella parked the car in a long, narrow parking lot lined with pine trees at the base of the Hill and breathed deeply, composing herself. In heels and a dress, she got out of the car anything but gracefully, instantly thinking she had made the right choice in not handing the car over to a valet at the top of the Hill. However, as she walked across the lot and up the staircase cut in the side of the Hill to the long, concrete steps alongside the road up to the Palace, she realized she was not wearing the proper footwear for such a trek. Leaning on a lamppost, she unzipped and slipped off her heels and stood barefoot on the cold concrete. Though she could feel its roughness, she could not feel its coldness. The snow had tapered off, but she noticed what flurries came her way melted before hitting her.

By the time she passed through the gate, the guard tipping his hat to her in his booth, her feet were dirty from the climb, sand having been thrown down on the steps. Betting she could wash them in the conservatory as opposed to dragging them through the snow, and hoping it was unlocked, she headed over to the glass building. As there was no sun these days, it was lit from the inside by magical balls of light Cinderella saw floating near the ceiling. The conservatory was unlocked. Entering, she was awed. Cinderella was used to pine and birch, but the trees in the conservatory had the largest leaves of the most vibrant greens she had ever seen. She walked among them in the heavy air trying to read their names and native origins. The scientific nomenclature made no sense to her, and some places she didn't even recognize. At the back was the entrance to the greenhouse. Peering through the window on the locked door, she saw row after row of tables with potted plants extending before her. Never in her life had she seen so much green at once, and she became jealous of the royals and those who lived in warmer climates. She walked back through the conservatory having forgotten why she was even in it, but stepping on a twig with her bare foot brought her back to her senses, and she quickly spied a coiled hose partially hidden beneath a purple-flowering bush of enormous leaves near the entrance where a cabinet and paper towel dispenser hung above a small trash can. She gathered some paper towels, and pulling out the hose and leaning against a tree whose curved, elongated green fruit hanging in clusters she did not recognize, she sprayed her feet clean, dried them, and slipped her shoes back on.

Exiting the conservatory, she continued up the sidewalk to the Palace. She had never seen the building in person before. It was constructed of fiery-colored brick and turned out to be smaller than she had expected. Photographs made the Palace appear so grand; to Cinderella, it looked dinky. She looked across to the Tower, likewise of brick, as she neared the valet attendants, hoping they would not recognize her. The Tower she found to be far more grand in its simplicity.

"Good evening, miss," a valet attendant said.

She forced herself to turn and face the young man as he tipped his hat to her. "Good evening," she said.

"The entrance to the courtyard is just ahead to the right," he said.

Cinderella had assumed she would enter the courtyard through the Palace, but a wide walkway ran between the Cathedral and the Palace, and there she took a right where the statue to the Princess, killed in the dragon attack twenty years ago, stood. At its base, many fresh flowers had been laid.

Cinderella heard mingling and music as she walked, the ground sloping up slightly. She grew nervous as she approached the archway entrance to the courtyard, doubting why she was even at the Ball. She knew no magic. She would make a fool of herself with the Orb in front of all these people. She slowed her pace, thought about turning around.

"Good evening, miss," a palace servant said and bowed.

"Good evening," Cinderella said. She didn't know whether to bow or curtsey or do nothing at all.

"I'm afraid they've just returned the Orb to the Chapel," the servant began.

Cinderella's heart sank. She had spent too much time fussing with where to park and looking around in the conservatory and had missed her opportunity to commune with the Orb. A moment ago she was doubting herself. Now, she was angry at herself.

"But," the servant continued, "you'll find it just inside after entering the transept to your left."

"I'm sorry, what?" Cinderella asked.

"You'll find the Orb just inside the Cathedral entrance to your left," the servant said.

"Thank you," Cinderella said, relieved she had not missed her chance to commune with Orb.

Before entering the Cathedral, she surveyed the courtyard, the space formed by the Palace, the Cathedral, and another L-shaped building. Not that many people were gathered, and there was no sight of her stepmother and stepsisters. She grew worried they had already left and would find her not home and the fire not lit. "Has everybody already left?" she asked.

"No, miss," said the servant. "Many lingered in the dining hall after dinner. Many are also touring the Palace. The dancing will resume shortly. I assure you, the party is just starting." He smiled.

"Thank you," Cinderella said. She made her way to the left, the tiles at her feet far more worn than those now behind her. Entering the wing of the Cathedral which housed the Orb, she was amazed at how brightly lit the corridor was. The carpet was red, the walls were white, moody paintings in elaborate frames hanging on them, and gold trimmed everything. She thought for a second she had mistakenly entered the Palace, that the servant had meant his left, not hers, though she recognized the events depicted in the paintings as religious in nature.

"Is this the Cathedral?" she asked an old wizard sitting on a bench reading a book.

The old wizard looked up from the book. He set his book down. Then he slid his masquerade mask down, taking a moment to adjust it. Then he stood up. "Yes, young lady, you are here to commune with the Orb."

Cinderella wasn't sure if it was a statement or a question. "Yes," she said. "I'm not too late, am I?"

"No, of course not," said the old wizard. "I'll have a servant find the High Sorcerer."

Cinderella grew embarrassed. "I don't want to inconvenience anyone," she said.

"Don't be foolish," the old wizard said, picking a black phone on the wall off its hook. "Please ask the High Sorcerer to come to the Cathedral," the old wizard said into the receiver. "We have a young lady who wishes to commune with the Orb. Thank you," he said after a pause, and returned the phone to its hook. "The High Sorcerer will be here shortly," he said turning to Cinderella.

"Thank you," she said.

The two stood in silence.

"I thought for a second I had entered the Palace," Cinderella said.

"Oh?" asked the old wizard.

"I wasn't expecting the Cathedral to be this elaborate," Cinderella said.

"Ah," said the old wizard.

They stood in silence.

The door to the courtyard opened, and the High Sorcerer entered the transept. "Good evening," he said as he approached Cinderella. He didn't wear a mask.

"Good evening, High Sorcerer," Cinderella said. She curtsied. "I hope I haven't inconvenienced you arriving so late?"

"Of course not," the High Sorcerer said. He motioned for her to follow.

As they started to walk, Cinderella was aware by the music drifting down the corridor that the doors had opened, and that by their whispering, people were entering the Cathedral and following them. To their right, near the doors that would bring them into the nave of Ianus Cathedral, a lengthy chapel stretched, unfurnished except for the Orb resting in a three-legged stand of gold. Just outside the chapel, a ledger, pen, and metal box sat on a small table.

"Your name, please?" the old wizard asked, picking up the pen.

"I thought this was a masquerade ball?" Cinderella asked, looking to the High Sorcerer and then to the twenty masked quests that had followed them to the chapel.

"It is," said the old wizard. "But we must of course know the names of all who commune for when the new apprentice is announced. It's okay if you don't have your identification card. I'll only need it later if you're selected. Along with your birth certificate. Your education transcripts. Employment history. Etcetera. There will be much paperwork to fill out," he said happily.

Cinderella looked over the gathered guests in their masks, suits, and gowns, her mind dizzy and forgetting what her stepmother and stepsisters had worn. More people joined them.

"Your name, please?" the old wizard asked again.

"Fiona," Cinderella blurted out. She then felt stupid, for if indeed she would be chosen as the new apprentice, they would have this fake name down and not her real name, but she was so scared to use her real name for fear of her stepmother and stepsisters. She was unsure why she was so scared, and she thought about correcting the name, but the old wizard had written it down in the ledger, and she worried if she said something then they would bar her from communing with the Orb.

"And this is your first time before the Orb," the old wizard said.

"Was that a question?" Cinderella asked.

"I'm sorry?" asked the old wizard, looking up from the ledger.

"Yes, this is my first time before the Orb," Cinderella said.

"Very good, Fiona," the old wizard said. He did not look back to the ledger.

Cinderella quickly scanned the crowd that had gathered. She was sweating. She looked to the High Sorcerer, who was looking at her oddly, as if he knew she had lied. Cinderella grew frightened that he was going to deny her access to the Orb, call security and throw her out for being a liar.

"Be calm, dear," the High Sorcerer said.

Cinderella nodded, but her eyes began to sting, and she wanted to cry. She turned away from them all and faced the Orb. She wanted to run away and forget all this. She didn't even know what she was supposed to do. The Orb tested her imagination, she knew that. She had to imagine something, but she didn't know what. She had heard Morta talk about volcanic mountains and rivers of lava, but she didn't know why.

"Please show us a scene when you're ready, dear," the High Sorcerer said.

Chapter 7

Cinderella stepped into the chapel. The crowd moved forward and closed her in. She was a liar, and now she felt like a fraud. She had no business being there, she felt. She had never even owned a training orb much less worked any real magic, and now she was before the Orb on Sigillaria. She had to show them a scene, but she didn't know how. All she knew was people "communed" with the Orb, whatever that meant.

The Orb sat in its stand like a globe, silver and featureless except for a slit on what was assumed its top. Cinderella knew there was some controversy over the nature of that slit, but she knew not what. She was nervous, but, taking deep breaths, she forced herself to stop. She had no reason to be nervous, she thought. And that was enough. Calm began to take over. She shifted her attention back to the Orb. No fingerprints were on it. It looked so pristine, but Cinderella felt it was only natural that she should touch it, and so she slowly and gently laid her hands, first her left, then her right, on the Orb.

The metal was warm to the touch. Pleasure touched her mind. Ecstasy embraced her. Then the Orb was cold, and her mind filled with terror. She yanked her hands away, backing away from the Orb as if to get away.

"Please continue," the High Sorcerer said.

Cinderella wasn't sure she wanted to. Curiosity won over. She knew the Orb couldn't be dangerous. If it was, why let the young access to it? she thought. Then she remembered she had no training and that maybe the Orb was dangerous to her uneducated self. Fighting back those thoughts, she mustered the courage to touch the Orb again.

The metal was cold. It stung. A jolt of horror struck her mind. She felt herself shivering. Pain overcame her. She opened her mouth to scream, but no sound came out. She thought she would collapse to the ground in agony, yet she felt herself falling forward. She lost concept of time. Darkness spread as despair engulfed her. For a second she knew fear unlike any she had ever known. Every previous moment became trivial in that one. Then it stopped. Relief poured over her mind. It was green. It was not peace she knew; it was something better.

She heard the gathered crowd whispering loudly in excitement. She opened her eyes. Large green streams of smoke were spilling out of the Orb. She closed her eyes and touched the green streams with her mind. She became aware that she could craft with them. Unconnected images from her life flashed through her mind, ending with the conservatory. She tried to recreate what she had seen there, but the image was vague. She got creative with it.

The crowd gasped in unison. Cinderella opened her eyes. In the chapel before her, she had conjured a scene of a brown path cutting across lush, green grass from which trees had erupted and risen from the ground on either side of the path, causing the gasps. Only apparitions, they took shape now, each resembling the tree with the curved, elongated fruit Cinderella had leaned against in the conservatory. Her focus on the scene before her, the detail of scene became stronger. The path she was dissatisfied with. In her mind she heard water, and she transformed it into a brook. Water trickled down the stony stream towards her. Applause broke out behind her.

"Very impressive, dear," the High Sorcerer said.

Cinderella took in the scene she had created,

then lifted her hands from the Orb. The image grew gray then dissolved into the air. She turned. The High Sorcerer was smiling. She made to take a step forward, but found her body too heavy, and she stumbled. A young man from the crowd rushed forward and caught her.

"I need to sit down," Cinderella said.

The young man helped her to the nearest bench, the crowd moving out of their way but not dispersing.

"Thank you," Cinderella said, looking up and seeing he wore a mask of red.

"Will you be alright?" he asked her.

"I'll be fine," she said. "Just feel a little drained is all."

"Should I get a doctor?" he asked.

Cinderella laughed. "No, I'm okay. It's just been a long day," she said.

The man in the red mask nodded. He walked off to where the High Sorcerer stood. The two of them left the Cathedral together, the High Sorcerer nodding to Cinderella as they passed.

As she sat there, recovering, for indeed she found herself fatigued, members of the crowd came up to her one by one, congratulating her, telling her how beautiful the scene was. They were all older. None of those her age came near her, and, recognizing her stepsisters, she quickly looked down as they passed her. Her stepmother did not come up to congratulate her. For that Cinderella was grateful.

"Wow, Fiona," said the old wizard coming up as the last of the crowd finished congratulating her. "That was incredible," he said, smiling.

Cinderella smiled back.

"This is for you," he said, holding out a small bauble on a chain. Cinderella lowered her head forward, and the old wizard brought the chain down over it. "May the warmth of the Orb go with you," he said.

"Thank you," Cinderella said. "It wasn't exactly warm though. Just at first."

"Oh?" the old wizard asked.

Cinderella nodded to the old wizard, then examined the red bauble. She didn't even own a training orb, and now she had been given a magical trinket.

"Everyone who has communed with the Orb this evening has been given one of those," the old wizard began. "It's a simple cold-warding bauble, but it's been enchanted for this evening. The red of the bauble will turn to silver for the new apprentice when he or she is selected tonight. That very well might be you."

"Was what I did really that good?" Cinderella asked.

"Young lady, magic like that hasn't been seen here in quite some time," the old wizard said.

Cinderella smiled. "Really?" she asked.

"Not even the High Sorcerer could conjure flowing water when he first came before the Orb," the old wizard said. "Truly you are gifted."

"Thank you," Cinderella said.

"Now, if you'll excuse me," said the old wizard, "I have to get back to my book. There's a whole series, and I'd like to have it done before I die."

"What's the series?" Cinderella asked.

"*Imaginary Gardens*," the old wizard said.

"I've heard of it, but I've never read any of it," Cinderella said.

"Highly recommended," said the old wizard. "My advice: start while you're young."

Cinderella smiled. "Okay," she said. She liked the old wizard. She wanted to ask him his name, but then she felt ashamed she had lied to him about hers. She grew worried what the repercussions would be if she was selected as the new apprentice, having lied about who she was. Then she thought she could pass it off as a nickname and felt a bit relieved. However, her mind jumped to the problem of having no magical training, worrying that if she was selected they would reject her. The old wizard had said they would need to know her education history, after all.

"Are you okay?" the old wizard asked.

Cinderella realized she had been staring off into space with her worries. "Yes, sorry," she said. "Just a bit worn out."

"Shall I get you anything?" the old wizard asked.

"No, I'm fine. Really," she said.

The old wizard nodded. "Excuse me," he said.

Cinderella sat there for some time, regaining her strength. Communing with the Orb had fatigued her mentally and spiritually, but sitting there was enough to adequately recover her faculties. Her mind frequently wandered to her worries, but each time it became easier to block her negative thoughts. Eventually, she became aware she could hear music faintly from the courtyard. The servant had mentioned the dancing would resume. She hadn't danced in years. She wanted to dance.

The old wizard, his masked pulled up, didn't look up from his book as she passed. When she stepped out into the courtyard, a polonaise was nearing its end. Many of those gathered turned their attention away from the dancers and towards her. She could feel their eyes, knew they were whispering about her. She felt embarrassed with so many eyes on her and insecure with so many words being said about her that she could not hear. She tried to ignore it all and focus on the music and the dancers. The dance came to an end.

"That was very impressive," a woman's voice said to her left. Cinderella recognized the voice as Morta's. Her heart skipped a beat.

"Thank you," Cinderella said, turning to face her stepsister.

"But you must know you won't be chosen on account of that magic," Morta continued. "The stream was a nice touch, but the scene lacked tension. Clearly mine was better."

"I'm sorry, I didn't see yours to know," Cinderella said politely.

With that, Cinderella began to doubt herself. She was clueless as to what kind of scene they were looking for. The old wizard had been impressed by the brook, but the High Sorcerer had said nothing about it.

"I like your tattoo," Nona said.

Cinderella grew alarmed, realizing the triskele

tattoo on her left shoulder blade was exposed, but then she remembered only Daphne and Daphne's brother, a tattooist, had seen her with it previously.

"Thank you," she said to Nona, relieved.

Nona's attention had shifted to the makeshift dance floor. "Oh my God," she squeaked. "Look who's approaching us."

Cinderella and Morta turned. The young man in the red mask who had helped Cinderella when she had stumbled was walking across the courtyard towards them. Cinderella stepped forward. She wanted to dance.

"May I have this dance?" he asked, offering his hand to Cinderella.

"Sure," she said. They walked together to the center of the courtyard where the dancers were assembling for the next polonaise.

The polonaise was the national dance of Amalthea, and Cinderella was familiar with all the music and variations in dance favored by her city, most composed and choreographed by Svetovid. At five, Cinderella had begun ballet and ballroom dance. She had excelled at both with dreams of someday performing with the national ballet company. When her father married Ananke when Cinderella was ten, her stepmother demanded that they end Cinderella's lessons. Cinderella demanded that they continue, and her father was all too willing to comply. However, as the years had passed and Cinderella's father succumbed to alcohol and depression, even he began to argue for ending Cinderella's lessons. At sixteen, she would have been able to compete with her dance school. By eighteen, if she had proven herself good enough, she would have easily found work as a background dancer with one of the lesser companies. But when Cinderella was fifteen, her father committed suicide. Cinderella's stepmother ended her dance lessons immediately.

Now at the Sigillaria Ball on her twentieth birthday, Cinderella began the march of a polonaise at the end of the procession with the red-masked young man. Full of energy and joy, she danced polonaise after polonaise after polonaise, even leading the last one she was to dance. At the end of it, her feet hurting and her legs aching, she excused herself, taking a glass of wine from one servant and bite-sized sandwiches from another, of which she devoured five.

She had hardly spoken with the young man in the red mask between dances other than to compliment him on his dance as many of the other dancers, male and female alike, had come up to him between dances to compliment him as well, some of the women hoping to steal him away from Cinderella. By the attention he received, Cinderella understood that he was someone of importance, but who he was she wasn't sure.

Exhausted, and finding she had many admirers of her own, Cinderella ducked into the Cathedral looking for a place to sit. The old wizard sat on his bench still reading. She thought of joining him, especially when she found that the other benches were all occupied by young couples in love or lust. Instead, passing by the chapel with the Orb, she opened one of the doors to the nave of the Cathedral.

Chapter 8

Cinderella found that the nave of the Cathedral was not as lavish as the wing from which she entered. The lights off, it was much darker as well. She had expected it to be cold, but with her dress it was not. Sitting in the first pew, she took off her shoes. The backs of her heels and the tops of her toes were red, yet no blisters had yet formed. Barely having broken in the shoes, she considered that remarkable. She sat there rubbing the aching bottom of her feet. The door opened, light from the corridor streaming in.

"I thought you went this way," the young man in the red mask said. "Needed to pray?"

"No," Cinderella said. She understood what he had said about praying was meant to be a joke, but she didn't laugh, as she laughed at very little. She could tell he was expecting a laugh. "I needed to take off my heels," she said by way of explanation. "I'm not used to wearing them."

"Ah," the young man said, advancing, the door closing behind him. He stood peering over the front of the pew. "May I sit with you?" he asked.

"Sure," Cinderella said.

The man walked to the central aisle of the Cathedral, then down the narrow pew, finally sitting at arm's length from her.

"You're an excellent dancer," he said to her.

"Thank you," she said. "I had lessons as a kid."

"And your communion with the Orb was amazing," he said. "I don't want to get your hopes up, but there's talk you're the one who's going to chosen."

"Oh?" she asked.

"Yes, that Morta's magic was very exciting," the young man began, "and everyone was talking that it would be her at first, but I don't think that's what the High Sorcerer is looking for, at least that's what I gathered from talking to him."

Unconsciously, Cinderella began rubbing her feet again.

"Do they hurt?" the young man asked.

"A little," Cinderella said.

"I can rub them if you'd like," the young man said looking at them.

"Are you any good?" Cinderella asked.

"Not as good as my dancing," he said. "But I've received compliments from time to time."

Cinderella turned in the pew and held up her left foot to the young man. "Very well, then," she said. "You may proceed."

The young man brought Cinderella's foot down into his lap and began to rub.

"So this Morta was the frontrunner until I showed up?" Cinderella asked.

The young man nodded. "Like I said, the High Sorcerer isn't exactly forthcoming with what he's looking for, and, ultimately, it's his choice, but my father did put in a good word for you."

"Your father?" asked Cinderella.

"Yes," the young man said.

"Who's your father?" Cinderella asked.

"My father the King," the young man said.

"Oh, you're the Prince!" Cinderella exclaimed. She grew red in the face. She made to withdraw her foot, but the Prince held it steady.

"Really?" he asked. "I thought the scar gave it away."

"The Prince has a scar?" Cinderella asked. "You have a scar?"

The Prince tilted his head to better reveal the scar on the left of his neck.

"Sorry. Didn't notice," Cinderella said. "How did you get it?"

"Acid accident," the Prince said.

"You should be more careful," said Cinderella.

"Actually, it wasn't my fault," said the Prince.

"A likely story," Cinderella said. "So, the King saw me commune with the Orb? Where was he?"

"In the crowd with everyone else," the Prince said. "He spoke very highly of you. My mother was there as well."

"What did she say?" Cinderella asked. Then she thought she had better ask the question more properly. "Did the Queen say anything of me?" Cinderella asked.

"Only that you have very nice legs," the Prince said.

"Thank her for me," Cinderella said. "Please?"

"I think I'll give you the opportunity to do so yourself," the Prince said.

"Oh, no," said Cinderella. "I'm far too shy."

"Actually, you'd be doing me a very kind favor if you did," the Prince said.

"How so?" asked Cinderella.

"Well, Morta has been here twice before," began the Prince, "and she has this twin sister. I can't think of her name. Norma? Nora?"

"Nona," said Cinderella.

"Oh, you know her?" asked the Prince.

"No," said Cinderella hurriedly. "I know the name. We have names outside these walls, you know?"

The Prince smiled. "Well, this Nona is a sweet girl and all, but she's gotten the idea into her head to make me her husband."

"Well, are you available?" Cinderella asked.

"My mother seems to think so," said the Prince. "I've always despised this day, but I've grown to hate it."

Cinderella opened her mouth to say it was her birthday, but she stopped. "I didn't even know you Royals could mix with commoners," she said instead.

"Oh, yes," said the Prince. "The Constitution permits a Prince to marry a Sigillaria Lady, the Princess, a Sigillaria Gentleman."

"But that's never happened," Cinderella said. She withdrew her left foot and, adjusting, extended her right.

"No," the Prince said, taking Cinderella's foot into his lap. "We're usually off marrying our cousins, but times have changed."

"Well, I wouldn't mind if times changed so much they abolished the monarchy," Cinderella said. "No offense," she added.

"None taken," said the Prince. "Actually, I wouldn't mind if it was abolished. Amalthea is ready for democracy."

Cinderella gave the Prince a look of disbelief. "But what would you do then?" she asked. "You'd have to get a real job."

"I have a real job," the Prince said. "I teach botany for the district's high school. Have you seen the conservatory?"

"Oh, yes," Cinderella said. "It's amazing."

"We have a banana tree there like the ones from your communion," the Prince said.

"Banana?" Cinderella asked. "Is that what that funny fruit is called?"

"You mean you didn't know?" the Prince asked.

Cinderella shook her head. "No, I've never seen that fruit before in my life. I stopped in the conservatory just before coming to the Ball."

"Interesting," said the Prince.

"What is?" asked Cinderella.

They could hear talking from the corridor. The Prince stopped rubbing her foot and pulled out his pocket watch.

"They're gathering for the selection," he said. "We should get out there."

"When do they make the selection?" Cinderella

asked, turning and placing her feet on the floor.

"Midnight," said the Prince.

Suddenly, Cinderella remembered she had to be home by midnight. She remembered Thanatos saying what she had forgotten earlier: that she wouldn't have time to dance.

"What time is it?" Cinderella asked in a panic.

"A few minutes to midnight," the Prince shrugged.

"Oh my God," Cinderella cried.

"We have time," the Prince said. "It's right there."

"I don't have time!" she cried.

Cinderella grabbed her shoes and ran barefoot for the corridor. Throwing open the door, she found a growing, noisy crowd blocking her way. She turned and ran, crashing into the Prince and sending them both to the ground.

"What's wrong?" he asked.

"I have to get home!" she cried, getting up. She ran down the nave for the doors at the front of the Cathedral.

"Why?" she heard the Prince ask after her as she shot through a door and down the stone steps.

Cinderella ran like she had never run before. She ran until her sides hurt, and then she kept running.

Skipping the long way to the gate around the sidewalk, she cut through the parked cars and across the snow, and though the magic of the dress and the bauble did much to ward off the cold, the snow was still chilling and painful. Coming out on the road, she stumbled, falling to the pavement and scraping her hands and knees. Crying, she stood back up and continued her flight, the guard not looking up from his magazine as she passed through the gate and down the road. Again, not wanting to follow the sidewalk down as she had followed it up, she ran through the snow and down the Hill. This brought her right among the pine trees, and she cut her feet on fallen twigs, needles, and pine cones as she passed through.

Her breathing pained her as she reached the car, rapidly typing in the keycode to unlock the door. Just as the lock popped up, the clock at Ianus Cathedral struck midnight, and the first of the twelve strikes against the bell began. Cinderella screamed in pain as the mask and dress dissolved into smoke, the cold tearing the life from her as she climbed into the car almost naked, the bauble at her breast keeping her warm. She turned the dial on the dashboard, but the car was dead, the magic gone. The windows began to frost.

From the backseat she grabbed the brown blanket and wrapped herself in it, panicked as what to do. Opening the glove compartment, she found a pair of her father's old gloves which she pulled on, finding them two sizes too big. She had tossed what she thought was her pair of high heels on the passenger seat getting into the car, but noticing now, only one heel was there. The other she had dropped, and she knew not where. Regardless, it had been the magic of the dress that had kept her feet warm on the concrete, and not even it had been enough to fend off the cold of the snow. Thinking that there had to be something in the trunk, she reached back and pulled down the seat and crawled into the trunk. It was cold enough in the cabin, but the trunk was colder. Sure enough, a pair of her father's old boots were there. She tossed them to the front of the car and rummaged through the rest of the items. Among the jumper cables, fuel can, tire iron, and rope, she found a few rags. Back in the driver's seat, she wrapped her feet in the rags and slipped on the boots, tying them as tightly as she could. Though the rags helped, the boots were still way too big, but they were something, and she was grateful she had been too lazy to ever clean out the car. Another rag she laid over her head, pulling it over her ears and tying it under her chin.

Cinderella didn't know what to do, but she knew she had to get home. Taking a tram would be the easiest option, but she doubted they were still running. Having never been out this late, she had never learnt the late night schedules, and it was a holiday after all. Another option would be to call a taxi as there was bound to be a terminal at the corner, but she didn't have her PDA with her, and it was busted anyway. However, she could use the terminal's pay phone if she could find some change. From the car's center console, she withdrew sixty-five cents, hoping it was enough for a phone call. Determined to get moving, she mentally braced herself for the cold, reminding herself she was a native daughter of Amalthea. Almost forgetting her shoe, she tucked the lone high heel under the blanket, opened the door, and rocked herself out of the car.

Cinderella found she could tolerate the cold, but she knew that wouldn't last long. She kept the blanket pulled tightly against her body, but it and the large, awkward boots limited her movement. Still, she pressed on, thankful there was no one out to notice her. Just as she came out upon the street, spying the terminal at the corner to her left, a tram clacked around the corner to her right towards her. Not believing her luck, she loosened her hold on the blanket and ran as fast as she could in the oversized boots to the stop, passing behind the slowing tram and quickly boarding the rear car at its rear door as it stopped. Through its windows she had seen that it was empty. She was thankful.

The tram resumed before Cinderella even made it up the steps, and she lost her balance and fell backwards against the door. She slid to the floor, her feet level with her head, the high heel which she had lost her grip on stabbing her in the back of her left thigh beneath the blanket. She had to roll to her right to get up, pushing herself up with her arms until she could back herself onto a step. The change and high heel fell to the floor at the door as she stood, the blanket hanging off her left shoulder otherwise exposing her. The tram slowed for the next stop. Cinderella was thrown down, nearly hitting her head on a vertical bar. As she lay there twisted, the door opened. She felt the heat escaping the car across her nearly naked body. The door closed and the tram resumed.

Quickly, Cinderella grabbed her dropped high heel, wrapped herself in the blanket, and took a seat. She hadn't noticed the number of the tram when she had rushed to board it, but it was the 12, and she was thankful for that. Relaxing, she noticed for the first time the car smelled strongly of alcohol and vomit, and then she noticed a bent-forward, passed-out young man in a seat at the front of the car. Eyeing the vomit, the smell only intensified for her, and she pulled up the blanket to cover her nose. After a few more stops, a group of young men began to board the car at the front, and Cinderella grew tense, but on smelling the vomit and seeing the passed-out drunk, they turned around and got off.

The remainder of the ride was uneventful, and a few more stops and it was hers. She headed for the park as quickly as she could, taking comfort among the trees and lampposts once she reached it, her mind relieved the trek would soon be over. She had survived. When she emerged from the park beside the hazelnut tree, her heart sank. The kitchen light was on, as were the upstairs lights. Her stepfamily was home. Cinderella was stuck outside.

She took refuge in the garage, entering the keycode on the building's door to the right of the garage door. The small space was cold and unheated, and she longed to be inside the house.

She could see puddles of oil and radiator fluid on the floor in the dim moonlight streaming in through the garage door's windows. Likewise, the garage smelled of it. Something scurried in the darkness. Pulling the stool out from the workbench, she sat and waited, too cold and exhausted to think or worry, staring out the window of the building's door at the house. The cold, darkness, and fumes as she sat on the stool gave her vertigo. She longed to rest her head on her pillow.

Finally, once the kitchen light went out, she waited for a few minutes then rushed to the back door at the kitchen. She entered the code and stepped inside. The warmth brought tears to her eyes. Sappho got up from her bed and approached her.

"Shhh," Cinderella said.

In the living room, the fire burned and, by the warmth and smell in the kitchen, had been burning. She had Thanatos to thank for that. It would be one less thing for her stepmother to complain about in the morning. Cinderella grabbed an unopened bag of crackers from the box in the cupboard and headed downstairs. The red glow from the *Fairyland Lost* title screen on her computer monitor was enough to see by, and the basement was warm, the space heater having been running the entire time she was out. She dropped the blanket off her onto the floor and tossed the high heel near her computer chair. The boots she pulled off without untying them. The rags she tossed on top of the blanket. She needed a bath now more than ever, but she slipped on her nightgown, ate half the bag of crackers, drank what water she had left in the kettle from her mug, and passed out in her bed curled up under the sheets.

Chapter 9

When Cinderella awoke, she thought it all had been a dream. Thanatos, the Angel of Death, showing up and giving her a dress to attend the Sigillaria Ball and commune with the Orb and then trekking across the city wrapped in a blanket and wearing her father's boots was all too absurd for her morning mind. It was time to get up and get to work, the way it was every morning when she awoke without alarm exactly at seven. None of it had happened. She moved. Her whole body ached. Which of course it would, she thought, after her work yesterday. It ached every morning. She remembered she had to take care of the premium channel box before her stepmother awoke.

But then Cinderella could feel something around her neck. Reaching to it, she realized it was a chain. She sat up, pulling the chain out from underneath her nightgown and examining the bauble in her scraped palm. The bauble appeared red, but then the room around her was tinted red in the light from the computer monitor. Looking to the floor, she saw the lone high heel on its side. So it all had happened, she realized, but the bauble was still red and not silver. She hadn't been selected as the apprentice. Cinderella peered closer at the bauble, rocking it in her palm. She couldn't be sure if the bauble was indeed still red or if it was the red from the computer monitor reflecting off silver. She got out of bed to turn on the light.

Standing up, her body sore and spots of sharp pain piercing her back, she heard someone walking upstairs in the kitchen in hard-soled shoes. That could only mean one thing, Cinderella realized: she had overslept. She pushed the power button off on the console, and the monitor went from the red of the *Fairyland Lost* title screen to black with a flashing green cursor. She heard the familiar drone of the news emitting from the television set on the floor above. She typed in "clock" and hit the Enter key, and the graphics of an analog clock themed to *Fiona in Fairyland* materialized on the screen. It was after nine.

"Oh shit!" she said.

"Cinderella!" her stepmother yelled from the top of the staircase. She began to descend into the basement. "Cinderella! Why aren't you up? Where's breakfast?"

Her stepmother flipped on the light switch. Cinderella saw that Ananke held the purple cable she had forgotten in the kitchen which she had used to test the Wedding Channel box. Looking to her stepmother looking at her, Cinderella found she looked furious.

"Have you been playing video games instead of working?" her stepmother asked. "Do you know what time it is?"

"I overslept," Cinderella began.

"And what is this?" her stepmother yelled, throwing the coiled cable at Cinderella.

"I needed it to check the Wedding Channel box," Cinderella said.

"And you left it on the kitchen counter?" her stepmother asked. "You couldn't put it away in the closet when you were done with it? Or aren't you done? There's another cable in a package sitting beside the television up there. Did you go out and buy that? How much did it cost?"

"I'm not sure," Cinderella said.

"Of course, because you know nothing of the value of money!" her stepmother yelled.

"We needed a new cable because the old one has gone bad," Cinderella said.

"But did you need to buy a Vesta cable?" her

stepmother asked. "That's a name brand. You couldn't buy a cheaper one?"

"I can return it," Cinderella said.

"On your own time you will!" her stepmother yelled. "And I'm docking you for two, no three, three hours pay. I'd order you to make our breakfast now, but you are filthy! Don't you bathe, girl? Do you actually live like this?" She kicked the blanket on the floor. "What are those?"

"They're my father's old boots," Cinderella said.

"You lie, girl. Is there a man in here?" Her stepmother looked around suspiciously.

"No," Cinderella said. "I was just going through some old things of my father's."

"To throw away, no doubt," her stepmother said. "We don't need that useless stuff cluttering up this house. I should make you throw away all that useless junk on those shelves of yours."

"It's mine," Cinderella said.

"It's my house," her stepmother said, approaching her. "You know, I should throw you out. You live here of my own mercy, you useless girl, and your attitude and defiance lately is really trying my nerves. Your father spoiled you, and look at you. Filthy. And no doubt a filthy whore!"

Despite herself, Cinderella had begun to cry.

There was only so much injustice she could take before breaking down.

"Such a—" her stepmother began, but stopped, noticing the bauble. "What is—. It was you! It can't be." Her stepmother looked down, noticing the lone high heel on the carpet. "The shoe!"

Cinderella looked to the bauble. In the light it was silver.

Her stepmother struck her. Cinderella stumbled back, falling onto her chair. She felt something wrap around her left ankle and pull her foot back against the leg of the chair. Then, the same occurred with her right. She tried to stand, throwing her weight forward and pushing up with her toes, but something came across her chest and pulled her down against the chair. It was then she realized the purple cable her stepmother had thrown at her was magically moving and binding her to the chair.

Cinderella screamed. "What are you doing?" she cried to her stepmother.

"You know, I've grown tired of that tongue of yours," her stepmother said.

As Cinderella had cried out, the cable had made its way around her mouth, pulling itself back between her teeth and keeping down her tongue. It circled around repeatedly until her mouth was filled with tightened cable. She struggled and cursed but to no avail. Her stepmother had gone to the top of the stairs. "Morta! Nona! Get down here!" she shouted. She returned to Cinderella. "You know, I think I should finally let Morta have her way with you. You've been sabotaging my family for too long, and now you've finally done it, you stupid girl."

"Where are you?" Nona called from the bottom of the steps to the second storey.

"In the basement!" Ananke yelled.

"What are you doing down there?" Morta asked.

"Hey, where's our breakfast?" Nona cried.

Morta started down the steps. "C'mon, Nona," she called.

"They still don't know who that girl who ran off is," Nona said from the living room.

"I hope they don't find her," Morta said. "They'll have to pick a new apprentice. I should be apprentice!" Morta shouted at the bottom of the steps to no one in particular. She looked to the bound Cinderella. She laughed. "What did she do now, mother?"

Ananke picked the lone high heel off the floor and dangled it from her index finger by the ankle strap. Morta's expression changed from amusement, to disbelief, to hatred. She stood there fuming.

Nona came down the stairs. "Hey, that's the other shoe," she said. "How did it get here?"

Morta jumped at Cinderella, grabbing the chain at her neck.

"No, don't!" Ananke cried.

Morta screamed as sparks flew. Withdrawing her hand, she had burns all over it.

"Mother, my hand!" Morta screamed.

"Why did you think you could touch such a trinket?" Ananke asked Morta. "Nona, go get the box with my rod."

"Hurry, Nona!" Morta yelled. Clutching her hand against her chest, she began to cry.

"You shouldn't have been so foolish, Morta," Ananke said.

Nona ran up both flights of stairs, but moments later she was back and standing at the top of the basement stairs. "Where is it?" she called down.

"Nona!" Morta cried and went for the stairs.

"You stay here and watch her," Ananke said to Morta, motioning to Cinderella, and setting the high heel down on the desk. She headed up the stairs. "Nona, I swear!"

"I don't know where you keep your things," Nona said.

"Why did you let the dog in, Nona?" Ananke asked.

"She was cold," Nona said.

After a few minutes, Ananke returned to the basement with her magic rod. "Hold out your palm," she said to Morta.

Morta did so. Ananke tipped the rod and held it so that the gemstone was in Morta's palm. A blue liquid poured from the jewel and engulfed Morta's hand, absorbing into it. Morta looked her hand over. It was healed. She turned to Cinderella and slapped her with it.

The doorbell rang.

Morta and Nona looked to Ananke. Ananke looked to Morta and Nona. "Are you two expecting anyone?" Ananke asked.

"No," both Morta and Nona said in unison.

Ananke looked to Cinderella. "You two stay here," Ananke said. "Keep her quiet. Here, Morta." Ananke handed her rod to Morta.

Cinderella saw Morta's eyes widen with devious joy. Ananke hurried up the steps as the doorbell rang again. Cinderella strained to hear what was happening upstairs. She heard a male voice, but the conversation was impossible to make out from the basement and with the television playing in the living room as well.

Morta had begun to play with Ananke's rod, and when Cinderella turned her attention back to Morta, a six-inch, blue blade extended from the gemstone. Morta waved it around.

"Be careful with that, Morta," Nona whispered.

"Oh, I'll be careful," Morta said, advancing on Cinderella, the blade pointed at her face.

Cinderella began to struggle and whine. Upstairs in the kitchen, Sappho pawed the basement door.

"Mother said to keep her quiet, Morta!" Nona whispered excitedly. She ran behind Cinderella and placed her hands over her mouth.

As Cinderella continued to whine, Sappho began to howl.

"Look what you've done!" Nona hissed at Morta.

Upstairs, Ananke could be heard in the kitchen. "Go outside, Sappho. Go outside! Stupid dog, go outside." Sappho began to bark. She was not going outside. The basement door opened. "Get back, you stupid dog!" Ananke shouted. Sappho whined, having been kicked. She pawed the closed door as Ananke descended.

"Who was it?" Morta asked as Ananke reached

the bottom of the steps.

"The Prince and three of the Royal Guard," Ananke said.

"What did they want?" Morta asked.

"The Prince said they're going to every household which received an invitation looking for the new apprentice," Ananke said.

"What did you tell them?" Morta asked.

"The truth," Ananke said. "That it was neither of my daughters who attended the Ball."

"Did they ask about Cinderella?" Morta asked.

"Of course," said Ananke.

"What did you say?" Morta asked.

"I told them she's off in Ophion on holiday and that it couldn't possibly be her," Ananke said.

Cinderella screamed at her stepmother through the thick cleave gag of cables.

"Did they believe you?" asked Morta.

"Of course they did," said Ananke. "Why wouldn't they? I'm an upstanding member of the community."

"Kinda weird they're on this side of town so early," Nona said.

"What are you going to do with her, mother?" Morta asked.

"I was telling Cinderella before I was thinking of

leaving that up to you," Ananke said to Morta.

"Me?" Morta asked.

"You do wish to be apprentice, right?" Ananke asked. "Perhaps you and Cinderella can work out some ... arrangement?"

Morta smiled. "Thank you, mother," she said.

"But not with the rod," Ananke said, outstretching her hand. Morta reluctantly handed it back to her mother. "Come up to breakfast when you've finished."

"Yes, mother," Morta said.

"Come, Nona, let's go make breakfast," Ananke said cheerfully.

"Wait. Why do I have to make breakfast and not Morta?" Nona whined.

"Because Morta has some work to do," Ananke said.

"You work today, Morta?" Nona asked.

"Come on, Nona!" Ananke yelled from halfway up the steps. Nona followed her mother upstairs.

Morta stood beside Cinderella looking at the cables and cords running down from and up to the ceiling. After a moment, her gaze shifted to the shoe Ananke had set on Cinderella's desk. Morta picked up the high heel and turned to Cinderella. "Where did you ever find such a pair of ugly shoes?" she asked. "When the Prince showed off the other one last night I thought I would puke."

Cinderella grew very nervous. She eyed the heel as Morta brandished the shoe.

"You always had such a small foot, Cinderella," Morta said. She looked to read the shoe's size. "You're a size six?" Morta asked in anger. She made a backhand strike to Cinderella's face with the shoe. Through the sting Cinderella was grateful she had been spared the stiletto, but Morta raised the shoe after the blow, and Cinderella stared up at the end of the heel above her.

Morta turned and swung down the shoe, bashing the heel against the desk until it broke off, screaming, "Such an ugly shoe! Such an ugly shoe!"

Cinderella's heart was racing.

"And where is that ugly dress of yours?" Morta asked. She ran to the wardrobe. "Where is it?" she yelled, tearing Cinderella's clothes off their hangers and throwing them to the floor. "It's not here! Where is it?" she asked, rushing to Cinderella's shelves and pulling the items to the floor. She scanned the clothes line. "Where have you hid that hideous dress of yours?" She came back to the end of the desk and grabbed Cinderella's bag. "Is it in here?" she asked, dumping the contents of the crossbody to the floor. "No? Where is it?" Morta screamed, and one after another she pushed off the electronics on Cinderella's desk, each crashing and breaking open on the concrete, the cables of some pulled out, the cords of others pulled down from the ceiling. Sappho began to howl.

Nona rushed down the stairs. "Are you alright, Morta?" she asked.

Sappho barked and whined. The basement door was slammed shut.

Morta pushed away the table at the foot of Cinderella's bed and flipped it over the shattered electronics. She eyed the desktop computer. "Is that ugly dress in that goddamn computer of yours?"

"Get back up here, Nona!" Ananke yelled from the cracked door, slamming it shut again. "Shut up, you damn dog!"

Morta grabbed Cinderella's computer mouse and yanked out the plug. Taking the cord in each hand she passed behind Cinderella, brought the cord down around her neck, and pulled. "Die, you bitch!" Morta yelled. She pushed her weight into the back of the chair as she pulled the mouse cord tightly to her sides. Cinderella struggled against the strangulation, but it was no use.

"Morta, what are you doing?" Nona cried.

"Shut up, Nona," said Morta. "I won't let this bitch steal my destiny."

"Nona, get up here!" Ananke screamed.

Cinderella was going to die. Her mind knew this, raged against this, but it could do nothing. Another part of her, however, came forward at that moment. It searched, and found in the darkness of everything the bright, burning azoth inside the bauble hanging from her neck beneath the cable that bound her. Cinderella felt the azoth with her soul. Her mind unleashed.

The bauble exploded, the blast directed away from her. The fire tore through the cable, and it fell, severed, to either side. Her nightgown, however, had been burnt through, her breasts singed. Her arms free but heavy, Cinderella grabbed at the cord at her neck with her left hand. With her right, she reached out. Her knife, on the floor, flung to her outstretched hand. The blade extended with the press of a button. Cinderella swung her arm back, driving the knife into Morta's neck. At the puncture, Morta threw her hands open. The cord at Cinderella's neck fell to the floor. Morta slumped to the floor, the blade tearing through her neck, the weight of the dragging body causing Cinderella to lose her grasp on the knife. She pulled the cable from her mouth. Morta lay motionless, blood erupting from the wound.

"Oh my God, Cinderella, you've killed Morta!" Nona cried.

The cable loose at her ankles, Cinderella slipped her feet out from it, but when she tried to stand and walk, she fell forward down onto the carpet, her legs and feet tingling, the sensation growing worse by the second. She realized she was shaking. Her ears were ringing.

Upstairs, Sappho howled.

"You've killed Morta, Cinderella," Nona cried, frozen in place.

Cinderella pulled herself up onto her bed, the sensation returning in her legs as she sat there. She looked to the knife in Morta's neck. She stood, walked, and retrieved it.

At the sight of the knife in Cinderella's hand, Nona slipped from her state of shock into one of fear. She put her hands out in front of her. "Don't hurt me, Cinderella," she said. "Mother, she's killed Morta!" she screamed.

Cinderella had no intention of harming Nona as Nona had done her no harm. However, she was not sure of Nona's intentions. Fearful yet to be feared,

Cinderella motioned threateningly with the knife to get Nona to back away from the stairs. As Cinderella headed up the stairs, her stepmother opened the door above. Her face filled with hate, the gemstone of the rod in her right hand glowing, she reached out with her left hand towards the knife in Cinderella's hand. Charging up the stairs, Cinderella grasped the knife tighter, expecting her stepmother's motion to wrench it from her grip. Instead, the blade of the knife shattered.

Cinderella drove nothing but hilt into her stepmother's stomach at the top of the stairs. Ananke had not had time to adjust her posture, and the force at which Cinderella plowed into her sent her down onto her back on the kitchen floor. Cinderella scrambled over her stepmother, but Ananke grabbed her leg, and she, too, fell down. Sappho howled. Cinderella could smell burnt toast. She stood, as did her stepmother.

As Ananke blocked the door out of the house in the kitchen, Cinderella ran for the living room. She heard the ice spell forming behind her. Sappho had stopped howling. She growled, and then Ananke screamed in pain. Cinderella felt the chill of the ball of ice as it flew past her. It hit the living room window and exploded, shattering the glass out. The heat raced from the house. Ananke screamed as Sappho mauled her. Cinderella flung open the door. She had to slam against the outer door repeatedly as it was frozen shut. She heard Sappho whine a horrible whine. Finally busting the outer door open, Cinderella stepped out onto the icy porch only to slip and fall, banging her head on the outer door, as Ananke flung three small shards of ice. They struck the outer door. Glass and ice rained down on Cinderella. Getting up, she made to run but slipped forward as a small shard of ice struck her back. The cold her body felt from the magic strike was far more chilling than the air and sidewalk onto which she fell.

"Help!" Cinderella screamed into the morning darkness as she stood again, her scabs torn off, her knees and hands bleeding anew. It hurt to speak. "Help!" she screamed through the pain in her face.

From the porch, she heard her stepmother's ice ball forming. Something came whizzing at her from the left. She heard her stepmother's ice ball release. Then her back was struck, but what struck her wasn't as cold as she had anticipated, yet it was far more heavy. The world spun as she was thrown down. Everything receded. She felt as if she was being swallowed by mud.

Chapter 10

When Cinderella awoke, she knew it hadn't all been a dream. A nurse stood over her.

"I was just adjusting your pillow. Welcome back," the nurse smiled.

"How did I get here?" Cinderella asked. All along either side of her jaw and up into her ears ached when she spoke.

"Do you know where you are?" the nurse asked.

"In a hospital, of course," Cinderella said.

"And do you know your name?" the nurse asked.

Cinderella found herself a bit agitated. "Cinderella. What's yours?" she snapped.

"I'm Zaria," the nurse said.

Cinderella realized she had a headache. "How did I get here?" she asked again.

"The Prince and High Sorcerer here, I think, are better at answering that," the nurse said, looking off to Cinderella's left. "I'm going to go call the doctor. You rest," she said to Cinderella. "Let her rest," the nurse said to the High Sorcerer.

At the door, the nurse knocked. It opened from

the hallway, and the nurse stepped out. The door shut. Cinderella thought that was odd. She could see the Prince staring at the floor as she began to turn towards the High Sorcerer, but pain stopped her. She groaned.

"Don't move," she heard the High Sorcerer say. "We'll come closer."

Cinderella heard the chairs scrape against the floor. The pain was subsiding, but her mind began to worry.

"Am I going to be okay?" she blurted out.

"You're going to be okay," the High Sorcerer said. "You were comatose for a little over two hours."

"Am I all in one piece?" she asked. She began to panic. "I remember trying to get away. To open the outer door. It was frozen shut." She tried to sit up, to inspect her body, but she didn't have the energy for it.

"You're all in one piece, Cinderella" the High Sorcerer said. Cinderella began to relax. "You're lucky the Prince and the Guards reached you in time."

"I hope you'll forgive me?" the Prince said, looking up.

"Forgive you for what?" Cinderella asked.

"Though we suspected it was you, and though we felt your stepmother was acting oddly, we didn't yet have grounds to enter her home," the Prince said. "We were at the terminal at the corner requesting your travel records – your stepmother said you were on holiday in Ophion – when we heard the window shatter."

"It's okay," Cinderella said. "I'm just glad you suspected me."

The Prince only nodded.

"It was the Prince's earth spell which stopped the brunt of your stepmother's ice," the High Sorcerer said.

"I'm sorry it wasn't enough to stop her spell completely," the Prince said.

"I'm alive, aren't I? It's okay," Cinderella said. "Where is my stepmother now?"

The door opened, and the doctor and nurse came in. Though medicine and magic had once each been their own fields, by Cinderella's time in Amalthea they had joined, and Cinderella was interested to hear that the doctor whose care she was under had been selected as the apprentice of the High Sorcerer ten years ago and afterwards had had extensive training as a chemist at the Tower and then healer at the Academy.

From a side pocket of his scrubs, the doctor withdrew a small device not unlike Cinderella's PDA but with three tiny gemstones affixed to the top of it. He began to scan her body with it, one after another the gemstones bathing her in their purple, green, and then red light. He asked her a series of questions attempting to discover the boundaries of her memory loss and her state of mind, finding her retrograde amnesia to be minor. She was showing signs of anxiety, but how much of that could be attributed to the head trauma was hard to say with everything considered. They wanted to monitor her over the course of the day in case of anterograde amnesia, but due to his scans, the doctor highly doubted it would develop. The salve they had administered while she was comatose was rapidly working. The ice shard which struck her back had been inconsequential, though Cinderella begged to differ. However, had the ice ball not been weakened by the Prince, she most likely would be dead if the ice had spread through her body. Everyone in the room considered Cinderella very lucky.

As the doctor was finishing up, a police detective arrived, and despite the protests of the doctor and nurse who insisted Cinderella needed rest and should not be bothered with such formalities now, Cinderella wished with the detective to give her testimony of the events. Though the doctor pointed out Cinderella was not the best judge of her condition, Cinderella argued that she was, and getting the story out now would enable her to rest later. The Prince called for an attorney.

Cinderella recounted the events of the morning, from her awakening to her stepmother magically tying her up with the cable to being left alone with Morta, the police detective recording the session on his portable tape recorder which he placed on the overbed table, the attorney taking notes on his PDA. The explosion of the bauble and the retrieval of the knife Cinderella explained to the best of her understanding, looking to the High Sorcerer for support. He offered nods, as he understood the power behind that which she did not.

She began to cry when she reached the part where she swung her arm back and the knife into Morta's throat.

"Is she dead?" she asked the detective.

"Yes," the detective said.

"I never wanted to be somebody to kill somebody," Cinderella cried. "But she was trying to kill me!"

"It was self-defense, dear," the High Sorcerer said. "Everyone can see that."

The Prince and doctor nodded; the police detective and attorney sat motionless. Cinderella continued on, ending with trying to get out the frozen door as the remaining events had been lost to her.

"What happened to them all?" Cinderella asked.

"Nona is in custody and is cooperating," the detective said. "Your story matches her story, and I can't imagine there being any problems in the eyes of the Law," he said, turning to the attorney. "Especially," he continued, turning back to Cinderella, "since the Prince and three of the Royal Guard witnessed your stepmother trying to kill you. In fact, saved you from an attack made against you by your stepmother."

"Nona didn't do anything wrong," Cinderella said. "Please don't let anything bad happen to her," she pleaded. "She's not like them." No one reacted, and she turned to the Prince.

"We'll see what we can do," the Prince said.

"She just couldn't stand up to them is all," Cinderella said. "Is Sappho okay?"

"The dog?" the detective asked. "Yes, she's in a shelter for the time being." The detective paused.

"As for your stepmother," he began, "she's still at large."

"What?" Cinderella asked, looking to the Prince.

"We didn't catch her," the Prince said.

"There is a manhunt out for her now," said the detective. He looked to his watch.

Cinderella was dizzy. She was afraid.

"We have an officer stationed outside your door and the Royal Guard have the hospital secured," the detective said. "Don't worry. She wouldn't dare come here."

The room was too warm. Something started to beep beside her. She needed oxygen. The room was spinning. The doctor called for the nurse as he brought the oxygen mask to her face. It had all been too much for Cinderella. She closed her eyes and fell asleep.

When she awoke, only the High Sorcerer was with her in the room.

"Have they caught my stepmother yet?" she asked.

"No," said the High Sorcerer.

"How could they not?" Cinderella asked, perturbed. She found the controls to adjust the bed. "How did the Prince and the Royal Guard let her get away?" she asked, bringing up the bed into a sitting position.

"Ananke is good at concealment and teleportation," the High Sorcerer said. "I should know. I trained her."

"My stepmother was your apprentice?" Cinderella asked.

The High Sorcerer nodded. "Yes, unfortunately," he said. "Do not worry about her, though. Concealment and teleportation are expensive magic, and, eventually, she'll run out of resources or make a mistake."

Cinderella's stomach growled. "I'm hungry," she said.

The High Sorcerer nodded and got up. He knocked on the door, and it opened. "Nurse?" he called. "Cinderella is awake and requesting food," he said lightly after a moment. "Thank you," he said to the nurse, and "Thank you, officer," he said to the guard. The door closed.

"The nurse is getting you a meal," the High Sorcerer said, returning to his chair.

"Thanks," Cinderella said. "And that fast? I'm being treated like royalty."

"Please stop worrying about everything," the High Sorcerer said. "Tomorrow we will bring you to the Hill and begin your training."

Cinderella began to worry. "High Sorcerer?" she began. She wanted to say more but stopped, afraid to speak.

"Yes?" the High Sorcerer asked.

"I know no magic," Cinderella said. "I don't know if I can even do magic."

"What are you talking about?" the High Sorcerer asked.

Cinderella grew red in the face, thinking it a serious question. "I've had no magic schooling. None. I just turned twenty yesterday. I don't even own a training orb. You might be making a mistake with me."

"Cinderella, I'm pretty sure you can do magic," the High Sorcerer said.

"But with the Orb," Cinderella began. She stopped. This is what worried her. She wondered how much of an influence Thanatos and its magic had over her communion with the Orb. The angel's magic had given her a mask and dress, had enabled her father's old car to run. She worried about how much of Thanatos's magic had played a role in the image she had conjured.

"What?" the High Sorcerer asked.

"Nothing," Cinderella said. She was afraid to

mention Thanatos. "It's just I don't think that my interaction with the Orb is enough to base my magical ability on."

"Ah," said the High Sorcerer. "Then let us consider your interaction with the trinket which allowed you to escape. And your summoning of the knife."

Cinderella nodded feebly.

"Do not doubt yourself, Cinderella," the High Sorcerer said. "You've had a horrible life, but it doesn't have to continue that way." He paused. "I'm sorry about your father."

Cinderella turned away. "Don't talk to me about my father," she said. "My life was going fine until he brought that witch into it. My life would have been fine if he didn't take the easy way out."

"Your father is a hero of the dragon attack twenty years ago," the High Sorcerer said. "He fought the dragon king Predator and blinded him in his left eye. Without him, I could never have gotten close enough to Predator to work the magic I did at that range. I'm sorry we didn't get your father the mental help he deserved."

"Whatever," Cinderella said. "I heard you had your own problems."

"When?" the High Sorcerer asked.

"I heard they called for your head," Cinderella said.

The High Sorcerer laughed. "Ah, yes, with the Council shortly after the attack. I was stripped of my rank and jailed on charges of treason."

"Amalthea sure has a funny way of rewarding those who fight for her," Cinderella said.

"It was Predator's head they wanted," the High Sorcerer said. "The Council called for mine since I let Nemesis retrieve what was left of Predator's. They were worried he could be resurrected." He shook his head. "If they'd only seen it. Over half of his logic board had been destroyed. Most of the forward components had been vaporized. Predator was done for." He stopped, staring off into the past. "It was a good spell."

"Do you think the dragons will ever attack again?" Cinderella asked.

"Probably. War is their nature," the High Sorcerer said.

"What horrible creatures," Cinderella said. "Why did God ever create them?"

"No god created the dragons, Cinderella," the High Sorcerer said. "We did."

"What?" Cinderella asked. "Why? When? I don't understand."

"In your studies, you will learn much," the High Sorcerer said. "Humans created the dragons millenniums ago to do better what we did best."

"What's that?" Cinderella asked.

"War," the High Sorcerer said.

"But not all peoples war. Our city doesn't," Cinderella said. "We are peaceful."

"We are neutral, not peaceful," said the High Sorcerer. "There is a difference."

Cinderella's brain hurt. "I don't understand," she said.

"You will in time, and now it need not be. Rest now," the High Sorcerer said.

Cinderella adjusted her pillow. "Who's Nemesis?" she asked. "I've, uh, heard that name before."

"Queen of the dragons," the High Sorcerer said. "She succeeded Predator. Beyond that, we know very little. Be assured, however, she is just as murderous as her predecessor."

"I've never really thought about the dragons," Cinderella said. "I guess I've kinda taken everything until now for granted, you know?"

"Most people do," said the High Sorcerer. "And then they're surprised when something bad happens. Fear a dragon attack, Cinderella. Then maybe we can find a way to defend ourselves."

"What do you mean?" Cinderella asked. "We have the Shield."

"No, we don't. The Shield is useless," the High Sorcerer said. "No one has ever been able to figure out the composition of that acid the dragons used to penetrate the Shield at Northwall and, presumably, get through the shielding surrounding the Cable to Rhea. So, of course, no one has figured out a modification to our shields to resist such an acid."

"Really?" Cinderella asked. She was beginning to realize there was so little she knew about the forces that kept her safe, but she had always assumed this problem from the past had been corrected.

"Believe me, we've tried," said the High Sorcerer. "I've tried. But after the accident with the Prince, I was forbidden to try. All that remains now, at least officially, is a team in Ophion."

Cinderella shook her head. "I never knew that," she said.

"Most people don't," said the High Sorcerer. He looked to his watch. "And now, if you'll excuse me, I will be off."

"What? You're leaving me?" Cinderella cried. She had felt secure with the High Sorcerer there.

"There are matters to which I must attend," the High Sorcerer said.

"But—" Cinderella cried. "My stepmother—"

"Do not be afraid here. There is a guard outside your door," the High Sorcerer began.

"A police officer," Cinderella mocked. "What good is a police officer against my stepmother?"

"The Royal Guard safeguards the hospital," the High Sorcerer continued. "Besides, there are wards in place here which Ananke would not only have to detect but dispel. You are safe here, Cinderella."

She shook her head.

"I can return in the evening and stay with you through the night if you wish?" the High Sorcerer said.

She nodded.

"Good then. See you tonight," the High Sorcerer said.

He stood just as the door opened. The nurse brought in Cinderella's meal on a tray, and the High Sorcerer left. As she began to salivate at the smell of her food, Cinderella wondered if the High Sorcerer had known the nurse was just about to arrive. Forgetting her fear, she remembered her hunger, and eating the warm meal put her mind at ease. That moment, however, was short-lived, for she slept fitfully for the rest of the day, each time waking up from a nightmare. The doctor returned twice to check on her, and the shifts changed, a different nurse bringing in her supper. Cinderella tried not to worry, tried not to think about Morta or her stepmother, but each time she awoke she was aware she had been dreaming about them.

The next time Cinderella awoke, she was aware that she had not been dreaming. There had been some commotion in the hallway. She strained to hear. Her door opened. She recognized the silhouette of her stepmother at once.

Cinderella threw herself over the guardrail to the floor as Ananke's ice spell exploded against an invisible shield of magic at the end of the bed. Realizing what had happened, she needn't have reacted so drastically, but her stepmother, dazed, hadn't expected the ball of ice to explode as it did, either. Cinderella lunged at her stepmother, knocking her down and out into the hallway. She slugged her stepmother in the face, pain coursing through her own hand. Eyeing Ananke's dropped rod, Cinderella grabbed it, but sparks flew, and she released it in pain. She saw the police officer lay dead slumped against the wall beside her hospital room door, but she didn't see his virge. Weaponless,

Cinderella ran for the stairs just past the nurses station as Ananke rose. No nurses could be seen.

The panel on the wall to Cinderella's right covering the fire hose swung open. The hose leapt out at her, Ananke controlling it, and struck Cinderella as she ran, knocking her down. Recovering, crouched, she jumped for the wall as the hose tried to wrap itself around her. Unlike the cable in the basement, her stepmother was having difficulty controlling it. Cinderella grabbed and pulled down the lever at the coupling, water racing through hose, Ananke losing what control of it she had. The hose swung back as it filled up and straightened out, knocking Cinderella's stepmother to the floor.

Cinderella pulled the fire alarm. The steel bell above began to resonate, the piercing tone painful to her ears. She grabbed the fire axe. "Stay in your rooms," Cinderella shouted, unsure if there were any other patients down her hallway, her voice lost in the high-pitched alarm.

Ananke stood. Cinderella rushed at her and swung. As she had done to Cinderella's knife in the basement, so too did her stepmother do to the axe. Before Cinderella could complete her swing, the blade shattered, but the strike to her chest was enough to send Ananke down. Cinderella turned and ran for the stairs. Bursting through the door, she stopped.

As the door swung shut, Ananke plowed it open. Cinderella swung the axe handle, striking her stepmother in the face. Blood splattered. Ananke dropped her rod and staggered back into the hallway. The rod rolled past Cinderella and down a flight of steps. Cinderella swung again, missing Ananke as she dodged, but, off her balance, Ananke fell to the floor. Her stepmother disarmed and fallen, the stairwell door closed, Cinderella knew she had the advantage. She spaced out her grip on the axe handle and jumped on her stepmother, pressing down as hard as she could on her stepmother's throat.

From the landing, Ananke's rod flung up, crashing through the window on the door and into Ananke's outstretched, open right hand. The gemstone flashed blue. Realizing Ananke was once again armed, Cinderella threw herself off her stepmother just as she went to stab with the six-inch, blue blade protruding from the gemstone. Rising, Cinderella struck Ananke's awkwardly outstretched hand, disarming her stepmother again. Cinderella ran for the fire hose.

As she had expected, her stepmother retrieved her rod and began to form an ice ball. Discarding the axe handle, Cinderella picked up the fire hose. She aimed at the ice and opened the nozzle.

A shard of ice struck Ananke in her stomach, the magic in her robe unable to stop it. She bent over, blood dripping to the floor from her face. Cinderella shut off the hose, her heart thumping. Ananke didn't fall. She pulled out the ice shard, dropping it to the floor. Her left hand glowing green, she covered the wound with it.

Two hospital guards came running up the hall behind Cinderella. Her stepmother looked up and rushed through the door into the stairwell.

Chapter 11

They moved Cinderella to the Palace that night.

Her stepmother had avoided capture in the hospital. In fact, she had disappeared. The trail of blood ended just inside the stairwell. A member of the Royal Guard who was a floor below on his way up reported not seeing or hearing her. Up the stairwell and onto the rooftop they could find nothing. The body of two nurses lay dead at the nurses station. Another was missing.

Cinderella's hand had been healed and her hospital gown replaced. The High Sorcerer had brought with him boots, socks, and a simple but magical gray robe. When they brought Cinderella down in a wheelchair, she got a surprise that brought an enormous smile to her face. The Prince stood just inside the hospital lobby with Sappho on a leash. Cinderella bet she was as happy to see Sappho as Sappho was to see her. Sappho wagged her tail and licked Cinderella's face, and Cinderella noted it was good to laugh. She felt more healed and refreshed from the laughter than from any of the bed rest she had gotten that day.

Cinderella sat in the back with the High Sorcerer in the Palace car as they drove down the streets, Sappho sitting between them. "You were wrong about my stepmother's powers," Cinderella said.

"Ananke is clever, not powerful," the High Sorcerer replied.

"Do you have any idea how she got up to my room then?" Cinderella asked.

"I'm not a detective, Cinderella," the High Sorcerer said.

"I just hope more people don't die before she's captured," Cinderella said.

"You'll be safe on the Hill," the High Sorcerer said.

"That's what you said about the hospital," said Cinderella.

The High Sorcerer did not reply. Cinderella wasn't sure she liked the High Sorcerer's aloofness but knew it to be a trait commonly associated with magicians. She vowed to herself that she'd never become so detached from the world.

As the car circled around the top of Ianus Hill, Cinderella expected it to stop before the Tower, but instead it stopped before the Palace. She was quick to learn that no one actually lived in the Tower but that it only housed offices, classrooms, storerooms, laboratories, and a library. Before the Palace steps with Sappho, the Prince, and the High Sorcerer, Cinderella looked to the Tower as the Royal Guard drove the car past it to the garages beneath the barracks. Many of the Tower's lights were on.

"In fact, I think I'll head there now," the High Sorcerer said, "and check on my potion."

"Did the agbayun berries make it better?" the Prince asked.

"No, I think they made it worse," the High Sorcerer said.

"Perhaps then go back to my original suggestion that it was not a berry but a bean," the Prince said.

The High Sorcerer stood there lost in thought. He nodded. "Yes, I must head to my study," he said and walked off.

"What was that about?" Cinderella asked as they walked up the Palace steps.

"He's trying to reconstruct a long-lost elixir," the Prince said.

"Will it be of any use?" Cinderella asked.

"Of course," said the Prince.

The clock on the Cathedral struck nine as they ascended the Palace steps.

"It was called 'panacea,'" the Prince said. "It's a

remedy for all disease."

"Pretty remarkable," Cinderella said, but her attention had been drawn to the extravagance of the Palace's foyer. She had never been exposed to such luxury. Gold and red dominated the room. She followed the pillars up to the ceiling where was painted an epic battle between dragon and human. She recognized it from books, one of the works of Perun.

"Watch your step," the Prince said.

Cinderella's attention was brought from the ceiling to the floor and staircase before her.

"I don't know what this is," she said, looking at the highly polished floor. "It's rock?"

"Red marble," the Prince said as they ascended the staircase, Cinderella focused on each step she took. "It's only found on one place on Terra, all the way down in the Southern Hemisphere."

"Must have cost a fortune," Cinderella said.

The Prince only nodded.

They walked down corridor after corridor and made turn after turn with Cinderella frequently having to tug on Sappho's leash. Finally, they descended a flight of stairs and exited the building.

"What?" Cinderella asked, confused as they crossed a short space in the open air and reentered the Palace. "Where are we?"

"The Palace is actually a collection of four buildings," the Prince said, "built – and rebuilt – at different times. This is the building you will be living in. Building D."

"But why aren't they connected?" Cinderella asked.

"It's something with how the Shroud is constructed," the Prince said. "It only covers the original building."

"What's this Shroud thing?" Cinderella asked as they ascended a far less grand staircase in a concrete stairwell.

"It's a magical barrier which protects the Royal Quarter of the Palace," the Prince said. "The Tower has one too. It's old magical engineering from when the two buildings were first constructed. There are generators deep in the Hill beneath the buildings. When activated, the Palace – well part of the Palace – and the Tower are protected by them. I can show you the generators sometime if you're interested in that kind of thing."

"Sure," Cinderella said, but she had to admit to herself that magical engineering wasn't very interesting. "But I think I'm going to need a tour guide for more practical matters first. I'm lost." The hallway down which they walked was less fancy than what she had seen in the Palace's Royal Quarter. Cinderella had never been in a hotel, but she had seen pictures of them when she longed for trips to Ophion. This reminded her of that. "Why'd they skimp on these Shroud things on the other buildings?"

The Prince shrugged. "I don't know," he said. "What I do know is my sister would be alive today if they hadn't."

"I'm sorry," Cinderella said, "but I don't know what happened."

"She was in the old Library when the dragons attacked," the Prince said. "With the Shroud activated over the Royal Quarter, she was trapped outside of it. There's an entrance to an underground shelter near the Cathedral. She was heading to that when the dragons attacked the Hill." The Prince paused. "I saw her die from a window. It's my earliest memory."

Cinderella wanted to say something, but she knew not what, and so she remained silent.

"A lot of good people died on the Hill that day when the dragons gutted and burned what they could," the Prince said.

"So, despite all that, they rebuilt parts of the

Palace without any magical protection?" Cinderella asked. They turned left at the end of the hallway.

"Oh, there's protection," the Prince said. "There's lots of magical protection on the Hill, far more than they had twenty years ago."

"Ah," Cinderella said.

"Here," the Prince said. He had stopped. Cinderella had kept walking. She tugged on Sappho's leash, but Sappho did not want to stop.

"Back here," Cinderella said and pulled harder. Sappho stood looking at her.

"This is your room. Room D dash 50," the Prince said. He punched in a keycode. Cinderella saw that the large pad was not numbers but letters. "To unlock your door, the password has been set to your father's name. You can ch—"

"Well, that was stupid," Cinderella said.

"I'm sorry, what?" asked the Prince.

"Nothing," Cinderella said, perturbed, entering the room first. She found the light switch and flipped it on.

"You can change the password on this panel here," the Prince said.

Cinderella looked back and nodded as Sappho walked into the room. Turning from the Prince, Cinderella surveyed the small, sparsely furnished space. There was a simple bed, a wardrobe built into the wall, and a small desk on which sat a telephone, pen, and pad of paper. Near it was a bed for Sappho, bowls, and a bag of dog food.

"The wardrobe has been stocked with clothes that should fit you," the Prince said.

Cinderella nodded.

"Your lost shoe is in there as well," said the Prince.

Cinderella checked to make sure the door near the wardrobe led to a bathroom. It did, but the shower had no bathtub. After the grandness of the Royal Quarter, she hadn't been expecting this. She felt cramped in the small room with the Prince and Sappho there.

"It's not much, I know," the Prince said. "The life of a mage. But tomorrow we can spend some time getting you what you need."

Cinderella nodded.

"If it's any consolation, the High Sorcerer lives just down the hall," the Prince said.

Cinderella nodded. Not on account of the living conditions, but on account of the presumed protection, that did console her. She took Sappho off her leash. Happily, she inspected the room and slumped in her bed.

"Breakfast is served from six until eight downstairs," the Prince said.

Cinderella nodded. "In this building?" she asked.

"Yes," said the Prince. "Picking up the phone will connect you to the Palace operator," he said, walking over to the desk. "My extension is 497." He wrote it down on the pad of paper. "Feel free to contact me if you need anything."

Cinderella nodded.

"We do have a kennel if you'd rather not have Sappho stay in this room with you," the Prince said.

"She's fine," Cinderella said.

"Okay," the Prince said. "Any questions?" he asked.

Cinderella shook her head.

"Okay," the Prince said. "I'll leave you be. Goodnight," he said, closing the door behind him.

Cinderella walked over to the panel and attempted to change the password for her door, but she could not figure out how it worked. Every time she thought she was changing the password, the display read "UNAUTHORIZED" instead. Frustrated, Cinderella gave up and walked into the bathroom. She opened the soap, inhaling the pleasant smell of lavender. Feeling refreshed after having washed her face, she thought she should take a shower, but she was too tired. In the wardrobe, she found a pair of fleece pajamas. She got into them, throwing the robe and her hospital gown over the back of the chair at the desk. She left her boots at the door. She pulled back the covers, flipped off the switch, and crawled into the bed. It was softer than she was used to. She closed her eyes and lay there. She needed slippers. Thinking she would get up and make a list of what she needed, she didn't and rolled onto her side.

Cinderella wasn't sure how much time had passed. She thought she had fallen asleep for a bit, but she hadn't dreamt if she had, and so couldn't be sure. The room was warm. She needed oxygen, but she found to her dismay that the window could not be opened, or, if it could, she couldn't figure out how to open it. Peering out, Cinderella saw the green aurora dance over the city. She looked down at Sappho looking up at her. "Let's go out," Cinderella said. As she slipped on her boots, Sappho got up from her bed full of energy. Cinderella threw on her robe and put Sappho on her leash. The two headed out to get some fresh air.

Almost immediately, Cinderella found herself lost. Thinking she was backtracking to the hallway with her room, she instead came upon a stairwell.

She took it to the bottom, finding a door to the outside. With Sappho before her, Cinderella stepped out into the cold, her magical robe keeping her warm. She took in deep gulps of the frozen air.

Taking in her surroundings, she was standing in a well-lit courtyard, but it was not the same courtyard in which the Ball had been held. To her surprise and delight, in the center was a small airship. A figure walked around it, inspecting it with a flashlight. Curious, Cinderella walked over. "Pegasus" was painted in black on the silver hull near the nose. The figure was inspecting the undercarriage of the airship. Beyond, a liquid azoth fuel tank with ten different types of hoses hanging on hooks on its wide front sat along the Palace wall. An abnormally large Network terminal stood beside it, seven sockets of different shapes and sizes on its face.

"Hello," Cinderella said.

The figure stopped and looked to her, and Cinderella was surprised to find it a woman. "Hello," the woman said. Sappho was eager to meet her, but Cinderella pulled her back. The woman resumed her inspection, shining her flashlight up into the stowing compartment for the front landing gear.

"Coming or going?" Cinderella asked.

"Going," the woman said.

Getting closer in the dim light, Cinderella couldn't be sure of the woman's age other than that she was some years older than her. Cinderella found her to be the most beautiful woman she had ever seen. "I've never seen an airship before," she said, taking her eyes off the woman when she realized she was staring and, blushing, turning them to the ship.

"Fascinating," murmured the woman. She ran her flashlight along the underside of the nose. Finished with her inspection, she shined the flashlight in Cinderella's face, then flipped it off.

Cinderella wasn't sure if the gesture had been intentional or not. Regardless, she stuck out her hand. "Cinderella," she said.

The woman didn't take it. "Oh? So you're the little lady who's been holding up my clearance," she said.

Cinderella overlooked the comment. She was more interested in the woman's accent.

"Andromeda," the woman said, taking and shaking Cinderella's still-outstretched hand.

"You're not from around here?" Cinderella asked as politely as she could.

"No," the woman said. "Beautiful dog. What's its name?"

"Sappho," said Cinderella.

Andromeda scratched Sappho behind her ears. "You are beautiful, Sappho," she said. "We don't have dogs like this where I'm from."

Cinderella took the opportunity. "If you don't mind me asking," she began, "where are you from?"

"Lots of places," Andromeda said. "Now, if you'll excuse me," she said, "I have some tests to run." She began to walk to the back of the airship. Cinderella followed her. "I've got a very long flight ahead of me, and I'm already behind." Andromeda walked up the ramp at the back of the ship.

"Oh, well, safe journey then," Cinderella said. The ramp began to rise.

Wondering who exactly the woman was, Cinderella reentered the Palace at the nearest door with Sappho. She found herself in a short corridor. Midway, a long corridor stretched to the right. Sappho pawed at the double door to the left. Peering through a window on the locked door, Cinderella found it to be the Palace kitchen. "C'mon," she said. Continuing down the hallway, they came to a door which led outside, and stepping out Cinderella saw the entrance to the greenhouse just ahead. It was brightly illuminated, and Cinderella noticed the Prince inside. She knocked on the door.

"Is something wrong?" he asked her as she entered with Sappho.

"No," she said. "I just needed some air and got lost and wound up here."

"Ah," he said.

Sappho bit and pulled her leash. "Stop it!" Cinderella hissed at Sappho. She turned back to the Prince. "Do you always garden this late?" she asked.

There were wooden crates stacked in a corner to which the Prince returned. "We got in a major shipment from one of our couriers this evening," he said.

"Andromeda?" Cinderella asked.

"Yeah. How did you know?" the Prince asked.

"I just bumped into her," Cinderella said. "Apparently my arrival had held her up or something."

"She had been waiting on me for some time," the Prince said. "Don't you worry about it. She was late in arriving anyway."

"What is that?" Cinderella asked as the Prince pulled a potted mushroom out of a crate he had just pried open. The white fungus looked as if it was bleeding red blood.

"Peckii," the Prince said. "Something the High Sorcerer ordered. Whatever you do, don't eat it."

"You don't have to worry about that," Cinderella said. "It looks so gory I wouldn't even touch it."

The Prince inspected the mushroom on a table on which sat other strange plants he had already unpacked. Cinderella wandered deeper into the greenhouse with Sappho. She could say with much certainty she didn't recognize any of the plants, although most were not as strange as the mushrooms the Prince was unpacking. She headed back to the front of the greenhouse. The Prince had opened a nearby cabinet. Cinderella eyed all sorts of laboratory equipment.

"I'm going to go walk some and then try to find my way back to my room," Cinderella said.

"May I join you in your walk?" the Prince asked. He set the mushroom he had just unpacked back down into the crate.

"Sure," Cinderella said. "But I'd like to go now," she said, motioning to the crates.

"That's what I meant," the Prince said. "This can wait until morning." Closing the door behind them, the Prince said, "We can walk atop the wall."

Sappho bolted, Cinderella losing her hold on the leash. Cinderella looked to see Sappho and a cat bounding through the snow.

"Sappho, come back!" Cinderella shouted. She started to run after Sappho towards the conservatory.

"It's alright," the Prince said. "The gate is closed. She can't get out."

"It's the cat I'm worried about," Cinderella said.

"I think that was Gyrinna," said the Prince. "She'll be fine."

"You don't know Sappho," said Cinderella.

"Trust me, you don't know Gyrinna," said the Prince.

Giving up on Sappho, Cinderella followed the Prince through the snow to the nearest tower. "Why are there no guards about?" she asked as they approached a door. "I always imagined the Hill would be crawling with guards."

"There're guards here and there," the Prince said. "There're guards at the top of the tower here, for example," he said, pointing up at the battlements with his left hand as he typed in a keycode on the door with his right. "But, otherwise, there's no need. The security of the Hill is mostly magical, unseen."

They climbed the steep, circular steps to the landing at the top of the wall and exited the tower. Cinderella was in awe as she looked through a crenel north, the city stretching out before her beneath the aurora in the sky. "It's beautiful," she said.

"The city or the sky?" the Prince asked.

"Both," she said. The Prince joined Cinderella at the next crenel as she leaned forward and looked to the east from hers. The walls of the valley were dark, but every so often she could make out a light. "Everything looks so different from here," she said. At last, and in a good mood, she decided to continue on. The Prince joined her at her side.

They heard the thrusters of the *Pegasus* start up, and they turned to look as the magical airship rose vertically into the air. It swung around to the south, its rear rockets igniting, and it got under way far louder and traveling far slower than Cinderella would have imagined.

"Well, I bet that woke up the whole neighborhood," Cinderella said.

"I had to give her special clearance to leave this late," the Prince said. "She was late arriving. Supposedly, there's some weird weather out past Typhaon. Weird even for them."

"I don't know where that is," said Cinderella.

"On the Echidna," the Prince said.

Cinderella shook her head.

"Surely, you've had geography?" the Prince asked.

"Surely, I have," Cinderella said, "but I was never any good at it."

They continued on in silence.

"Why did you rush off last night?" the Prince asked. They were just over the gate, halfway between the tower they had ascended and the next.

"Because I had to get home," Cinderella said.

"Yes, but why?" the Prince asked.

Cinderella walked and peered from a crenel out across the Hill to the Cathedral. "What time is it now, anyway?" she asked.

The Prince looked to his watch. "Almost midnight," he said. "You're not going to run off are you?" the Prince asked dryly.

Cinderella could see the clock on the Cathedral. It was a minute until midnight. Below, a figure was crossing through the snow from the Tower towards the greenhouse. "I think the High Sorcerer is heading to the greenhouse," she said.

The Prince joined her at her crenel. "Yeah, that's him," he said.

"Should we call out?" Cinderella asked.

The clock struck midnight. The Cathedral bell began to toll. The High Sorcerer had stopped midway in the road, looking about. There was an odd wind accompanied by odd mechanical sounds. Cinderella looked all around, but though she could feel and hear something, she could see nothing.

Then, the sirens blared, and the Hill lit up.

Cinderella watched helplessly as the dragon Nemesis decloaked behind the High Sorcerer. The dragon drove a claw through the High Sorcerer's back and out through his chest. She lifted him into the air, blood pouring to the pavement. "And so I have slain you," Nemesis said. "And so Predator is avenged." She tossed the corpse off her claw to the ground.

As Nemesis had done so, the magical security protecting the Hill had been triggered. Sirens sounded all across it, reverberating. Magical barriers draped the Palace and Tower in purple light. Four more dragons decloaked around the road as numerous magical balls of blue light materialized. They opened fire on one another: dragon fire against magic bolt. The light lit up the winter night. Cinderella stared into it.

"Get down," the Prince had been yelling

repeatedly. He dragged her drown.

At either end of them, the towers on the wall opened fire, lightning streaming into the courtyard. Behind the merlon, Cinderella and the Prince clutched one another as flame rushed over it and through the crenels. Cinderella felt the stone grow warm. She thought her time on Terra was at an end, but the Prince had called forth a magical shield around them which glowed yellow as the gemstone on his rod glowed red. When the fire ceased, the towers to the left and right were blasted with fireballs again and again, stone being thrown everywhere into the air, some of it raining down on them, the largest pieces bouncing off the shield, the smallest being absorbed by it. Cinderella could do nothing but stare into the red of the gemstone.

The sky to the north brightened in a white that pulled Cinderella's attention to it. Blinded by the light, even as it began to fade, she still saw its brilliance. The explosion came, Cinderella hearing it and feeling it through the stone of the wall. She fumbled to the outer battlements.

"Get back!" the Prince yelled.

Cinderella didn't care. The world was ending. She peered through a crenel to the north, spots of light still in her vision. The city had gone dark. An enormous, yellow pillar of smoke rose into the sky in the near distance. "The power plant," Cinderella said. She heard the Prince yelling behind her, but she didn't know what he was saying. Nor was she sure what she was seeing. Under the aurora, spots of light still on her vision, she could tell something dark and massive was flowing out across the city, down streets and through buildings, originating from the power plant.

The Prince had rushed across to her and was trying to pull her back.

"No!" she cried. "Look!" she pointed out through the crenel. "Look!" she cried again.

The wall exploded near the tower they had ascended. Another explosion followed, closer to them. The third struck their part of the wall. Cinderella fell, her ears ringing and eyes wide open. The Prince had wrapped his arms around her. A shield of yellow swirled all around them. Though she lay awkwardly on a pile of rubble, she was uninjured.

"You okay?" she asked the Prince.

"Yeah," he said. "You?"

"Look," she said.

Cinderella climbed down the rubble towards the city. As she stood up on the road down the Hill, the wave of dark light rushed towards it. At a storey high, the wave swallowed the first floors of the buildings of the Old Town, their two upper storeys untouched. Though it roared and flowed like water, it did not splash like water, and Cinderella watched as the gray darkness rushed not around but through the Hill. She stared down into it, thinking she was on an island in the abyss. She was not sure if the dark light was rising or the Hill was sinking, but she knew it was getting closer by the second. When she looked to the buildings of the Old Town, they were already deeper into the gray darkness.

"It originated at the power plant," Cinderella said, her gaze fixated on the unreal scene below her.

"Oh my God," the Prince said.

Cinderella turned back. The Prince hadn't climbed down the rubble. Instead, he stood at the top of it. In the light of the darkness, Cinderella could see the look of horror on his face.

"What is it?" Cinderella asked.

"They've created a gravity pit," the Prince said. He began to shake his head. "I don't know how, but they have. It's going to swallow the city."

"What?" Cinderella asked. She looked down to the dark light. "It's rising!" she cried.

"We're sinking," the Prince said.

From within the wall, Cinderella heard Sappho begin to bark. Then Nemesis was upon them. The dragon grabbed the Prince with her right claw. He lost his grip on his rod, and it fell among the rubble.

"I cannot believe my luck," Nemesis said. Walking on her hind legs, she carried the Prince away towards the Palace.

Whether the dragon did not see her or did not care, Cinderella did not know.

Chapter 12

Cinderella was unsure what to do. She climbed on the rubble, looking for the Prince's rod. She could not find it, and if she did, she wasn't sure if she could even hold it, let alone use it, after her encounter with her stepmother's rod in the hospital. She didn't know what to do. She didn't know how to save the Prince. She didn't know how to save herself. She looked down to the dark light as the Hill continued to sink into it. Perhaps, she thought, the magicians of the Tower could help. Then she thought of the Orb. Perhaps she could use the Orb to save the Prince. Perhaps she could use the Orb to escape the Hill.

Climbing further up the rubble, Cinderella thought she saw someone down the road. She stopped and looked, but there was no one that she could make out. She watched the road as the Hill continued to sink into the dark light. She had to move.

Back within the blasted walls of the Hill, Cinderella became aware that the sirens had been silenced. Neither the Palace nor the Tower were protected by the Shrouds. Cinderella remembered what the Prince had said about the generators being deep down beneath the buildings and surmised that the dark light had destroyed them. Parts of the Royal Quarter of the Palace were aflame, the three other buildings engulfed. Charred bodies and craters were scattered about. No magical blue balls remained. The glass of the conservatory was shattered, its trees ablaze. A firefight waged at the Tower between dragon and magician. Cinderella could see into the building for much of the outer walls had been blasted away. Parts of the Tower had collapsed. One dragon lay motionless at its base. The Cathedral stood untouched.

Twenty years and two days ago, Predator had not been prepared for the Shrouds, bringing his attack to a halt. With the King safe behind the Shroud, Predator had ordered the city burnt street by street until the King surrendered. He never surrendered, and for two decades, the actions of the King on that day had been debated by the people of Amalthea. Some argued him a heroic leader. Others called him a coward who let his people die. For her attack, Nemesis had made the

Shrouds her priority, eliminating them, along with most of Amalthea, with a new weapon she believed would soon bring humans the world over to their knees. Hunched on her hind legs and clutching the Prince in her right claw, she hurled insults at the defenseless Palace, most of them lost in the firefight at the Tower. From the diminishing sounds and flashes of returned fire, Cinderella knew the sorcerers were about finished.

Behind the burning barracks Cinderella ran. Ahead, something moved in the snow low to the ground. She thought it was an injured person at first but then realized it was Sappho. She whimpered and whined as Cinderella neared, but did not move. In the glow of the fire, Cinderella inspected Sappho for injuries, thankfully finding none other than the paralysis of fear. She gave Sappho the largest hug she had ever given her and removed her leash.

"C'mon," Cinderella said, rising. She started to walk towards the Tower. Sappho did not follow. "C'mon," Cinderella called again, turning back to face Sappho.

Sappho began to growl, then stood and barked.

Cinderella swung around to see a dragon making its way around the Tower. It took its attention off the building, looking past her to the barking Sappho. Cinderella saw its torch light up, but then lightning crackled down from the Tower above, striking the dragon on its back. The dragon turned to the Tower, unleashing a fireball.

"C'mon," Cinderella called to Sappho. As debris from the Tower rained down and the dragon streamed flame into the building, Cinderella ran through the snow past the dragon and behind and around the Tower, stumbling over wreckage repeatedly. She did not look back to see if Sappho was following her, but when she threw herself against the statue of Capricornus, Sappho was at her side.

Cinderella heard lightning from the Tower, then a fireball, then silence. The last defender was dead.

"Come out, King of Amalthea!" Nemesis shouted. "Bear witness to the dawn of a new age! Your defenders are dead! The Eigengrau is upon you! Nothing protects you from me! Look upon your feeble son one last time!"

Peering around the statue, Cinderella saw the Queen step out onto an upper balcony of the Palace. The King joined her.

"Mother! Father!" the Prince cried out. "They've created a gravity pit! You have to—"

"Silence," Nemesis said. She squeezed the Prince.

"No," the Queen cried, reaching out uselessly towards her son.

The King turned his attention to the city. The three dragons came up beside Nemesis. The wings of the one closest to Cinderella dragged limp on the ground.

"What horror have you unleashed, dragon?" the King cried out.

"You had your chance. Goodbye, King of Amalthea," Nemesis said.

Overkill, the other three dragons streamed fire onto the balcony on which stood the King and Queen. The flames took hold on the Palace and spread.

"The King is dead," Nemesis said to the Prince, now King, in her claw. "What say you? Long live the King?"

The new King said nothing.

"Nemesis?" the dragon with the limp wings said meekly. "The Eigengrau."

"Astraea. Svarog," Nemesis said. "Carry Phaethon to Northwall. Hellfire should be done there."

"What about Molok?" Astraea asked.

"I checked. He's dead. Leave him," Nemesis said. "I will join you just as soon as I'm done with our new King here."

Nemesis walked closer to the burning Palace where the statue of the Princess stood. Astraea and Svarog each grabbed Phaethon by a forearm. Together, the three dragons leapt into the air with the aid of their hind rockets. Spreading and flapping their wings, the two dragons carried the dangling third off to Northwall.

"I have a proposition for you, King of Amalthea," Nemesis said.

"You can offer me nothing, murderer," the King said.

"Your city is destroyed. Your nation wiped out," Nemesis said. "We will set loose the Eigengrau on city after city until your species surrenders to us. You can prevent this massacre. Become my emissary to your species, King of Amalthea. Share the tale of your city and my mercy. Persuade humankind to relinquish itself to the dragon."

"We will die before we live as your slaves again," the King said.

"I do not think your kind will resist for long, dear King," said Nemesis. "Join me now. Save yourself. Save the people of Naukratis and how many other cities from annihilation."

Cinderella saw the King look to the statue of Capricornus.

"No," he said.

"Fool," Nemesis hissed. She opened her mouth and extended her torch. "Die, King of Amalthea."

A brick from the Tower lay in the snow at Cinderella's feet. Without thinking, she picked it up and ran out from behind the statue. Nemesis dropped the King to the ground. "No!" Cinderella screamed. Sappho began to bark. Nemesis paid them no mind. Cinderella threw the brick, but her aim was bad, and it bounced off Nemesis's leg. The dragon rained down fire. From the ground, the King flung up a vial into it.

Cinderella wasn't sure what happened next. Nemesis's fire never reached the King. Instead, it was sucked back. There was an explosion, a flash of green.

"Into the Cathedral!" the King yelled as he stood. He ran limping towards Cinderella.

Cinderella looked to the dragon. Nemesis was maimed but alive. She stood there dazed, her lower jaw obliterated but her torch intact, the armor of her neck damaged and torn.

Cinderella and Sappho ran up the steps.

Cinderella stopped and pulled open a Cathedral door, Sappho panting and dashing past her into the nave. Cinderella turned back. "Get—" the King shouted, nearly reaching the steps.

Nemesis pounced. She caught the King by his dragging right leg. He fell forward, smashing his face against the first stone step.

Horrified, Cinderella screamed in spite of herself. Her insides twisted. Bile burned her throat. Nemesis looked to her, the dragon's torch lighting up as they came face to face. Cinderella turned and ran into the Cathedral. She broke right down a pew as the doors exploded. Fire, wood, and stone blew down the center aisle.

Nemesis entered the Cathedral and crashed through the pews after Cinderella. Unsure where Sappho was, Cinderella called out her name. Cinderella rushed through the doors to the corridor with the Orb. Immediately behind her, Nemesis drove her claws through the wall and pulled the doorframe down. Cinderella ran into the chapel and grabbed the Orb. Taking it off its pedestal and holding it to her chest, she felt its cold, dark energy. She stepped back into the corridor as Nemesis stuck her head down it. The dragon's torch began to glow. Barely realizing what she was doing,

Cinderella let loose with the Orb.

Thick, thorny, brown vines erupted from the Orb. They wrapped themselves around Nemesis. Cinderella could hear the thorns puncturing the dragon's armor. Nemesis thrashed as the vines extended beyond her into the nave of the Cathedral, dragging the dragon back and pulling her up above the floor between four pillars.

Ice struck Cinderella, her robe absorbing the magic. Cinderella turned to see her stepmother advancing down the corridor from the courtyard. She wanted to strike out at her stepmother with the magic of the Orb, but it offered her nothing, the vision of the vines in her head. Cinderella realized then the limitations of the relic. She ran back into the nave of the Cathedral. Sappho stood in the center aisle looking up at Nemesis suspended between the four pillars.

"C'mon, Sappho," Cinderella yelled.

Her stepmother rushed into the nave of the Cathedral letting ice magic fly wildly. Cinderella ran to the building's blasted out entrance and stopped. The Eigengrau had reached the stone steps of the sinking city's Cathedral. The King's body was gone. To Cinderella's left, the door and wall blocking off the bell tower stairs had been blown apart by Nemesis's fire. Cinderella took to the stairs, Sappho following, her stepmother shortly behind.

Cinderella and Sappho climbed much faster than Ananke. The distance between them increased even more as her stepmother periodically stopped to fling ice spells Cinderella's way. Reaching a landing, there was a door out onto the second level balconies of the Cathedral. Another led to the roof and belfry. Cinderella took the latter, Sappho at her heels. At the landing to the roof, Cinderella stopped her ascent. She plowed through the door and ran out onto the ridge of the roof. It sloped steeply to either side, the colorful tiles which formed zigzag patterns catching the light of the burning Palace. The design made Cinderella dizzy. Sappho had followed her, but as Cinderella ran across the roof, Sappho stopped and whined. In the middle of the roof, Cinderella stopped, unsure what to do, the vision of the vines in her head. She thought to take her hold off it and use the Orb against her stepmother, but then she knew she would have a very angry dragon loose below her.

The door was flung open. Ananke stepped out and stopped. Sappho tried to turn around to face her and attack but slipped. She slid down the roof, the four foot high parapet stopping her from sliding off. Uncertain how to fight, Cinderella ran. Ananke followed, throwing ice spell after ice spell at Cinderella's feet. At last, one caught her, and she fell forward, dropping the Orb. It rolled down the roof and, like Sappho, hit the parapet. Cinderella tried to stand, but her feet were bound together, encased in ice. Reaching out to the Orb, she tried to call it to her, but she felt nothing. She tried to roll over, but the weight at her feet she could not control. It started to pull her down the side of the roof, twisting her torso as it did so.

At the angle she lay, she could see her stepmother slowly advancing towards her. Sappho was trying to climb back up the roof, but kept sliding as she did so. The gemstone on Ananke's rod glowed blue.

"And now, Cinderella, be a good girl and die," her stepmother said.

The roof at Ananke's feet bulged, bubbled, and then ruptured. A pillar of flame gushed skywards, devouring Cinderella's stepmother. The ice encasing Cinderella's feet melted. She scrambled back as the roof caved in before her. As she stood, Nemesis awkwardly climbed through the hole. Cinderella turned and ran down the ridge of the roof towards the back of the Cathedral.

White light blinded her. She heard the roar of magical thrusters. The *Pegasus* was before her. Cinderella saw the barrel of the cannon light up. She threw herself down. The bolt of lightning streaked over the rooftop. Nemesis had seen it too. Jumping out of the way, she spread her wings and took flight. The lightning struck the bell tower, blowing out a three foot hole.

Cinderella ran down the rooftop at an angle to the Orb. "Sappho," she called. "Come to me." She looked back to Andromeda in the cabin hoping she had followed her movement.

Andromeda moved the *Pegasus* beyond the roof, then lowered it as the ramp at the back of the airship opened over the parapet.

"Lower!" Cinderella cried. "Jump, Sappho. Jump!" Cinderella cried when the ramp came to a halt.

Sappho would do no such thing. Cinderella quickly picked up the dog and hoisted her onto the ramp. As she couldn't climb up holding the Orb, she threw it over her head into the hold of the airship.

"We need to go!" Andromeda yelled.

Cinderella pulled herself up onto the ramp. As the ramp began to rise, she crawled, stood, then ran up it into the empty hold. Netting and hooked ropes and chains hung secured from the ceiling and walls. Sappho looked back at her from the cabin. "Go!" Cinderella shouted. "Go!" she shouted again, grabbing the Orb.

The *Pegasus* banked hard to the left. Cinderella fell against the wall, dropping the Orb. She heard the explosion and saw the flash through the opening as the ramp raised.

"Hold on!" Andromeda yelled.

The airship shot forward, and the Orb rolled to the back of the ship. Cinderella threw herself on top of it, sliding with it to the edge of the ramp. She could feel its power, but she wanted nothing from it. She only wanted to live. She lay there until the ramp sealed shut. Sappho came to her. Rising with the Orb, Cinderella made her way into the cabin and strapped herself in, Sappho curling up at her feet.

Andromeda flew fast and low with no airship lights over the frozen Undine following a route mapped out on a dashboard monitor before her. Cinderella looked to the five monitors on the center dash of the airship displaying darkness. She relaxed into her seat, the doomed city, the dark light, and the dragons left behind them.

"How did you know to come back?" Cinderella asked.

"The lights on the highway went out," Andromeda said, motioning to the right with a tilt of her head. "I thought something might be wrong."

"Thank you," Cinderella said.

Andromeda nodded.

The *Pegasus* sped south following the frozen river.

About the Author

Stephen Oravec holds a B.A. in Writing (2001) and an M.A. in English Literature (2003) from the University of Toledo. His hobbies include taking pictures, playing video games, and drinking coffee. This is his first novel.